THE LOVESTRUCK DETECTIVE

M.C. Anderson

A Big Muddy Mystery

⫻BookBaby

7905 N. Crescent Blvd
Pennsauken, NJ 08110
Printed in the United States of America.

MCAndersonBooks.com

For Sandi, with love and gratitude

"See how love and murder will out."

William Congreve

Prologue

It was a bleak time in a bleak place, and a bartending job and temp work was all I could get with America in recession. No one was hiring ecologists.

I was spending my off time on the Missouri or tramping along its banks. A working river, the "Big Muddy" shoulders barges and various watercraft of fishermen as it snakes through the middle of its namesake state, but despite its harnessing this sometimes broad and rather shallow stream remains a wild and untamed force of nature, and those familiar with it respect the power and speed of its swirling currents, knowing how hazardous it can be. Not a pretty river, it is, as its sobriquet suggests, a dirty waterway, collecting run-off from miles of farm fields and debris from passing through the industrial areas of Kansas City.

The body I discovered bobbing along its bank one April day hardly seemed out of place.

Just one more bit of human contamination.

1

The day began early. In the half light I pulled on a windbreaker, whistled for Buddy and, despite a chill wind, headed out the back door to the boat dock. I'd gotten a short-term state environmental contract to research the number and species of birds in a wetlands along the river, and dawn with the sun rising over the bluff made a pleasurable time to do my counts. Along the path to the dock, crocuses were poking their heads up through the dank earth, a reminder that spring had only recently arrived. I shoved the boat off into the creek, letting the outboard run just above an idle, taking time to indulge in the sights around me—the rising bank obscured by hardwood trees, the gentle current flowing around a branch that dipped into the water.

The mist started to retreat as I reached the creek's mouth, and when I entered the channel, the sun crept over the horizon and its rays danced on the water, creating a silvery surface that hid the river's bowels. The light show was mesmerizing,

but the powerful and swift-flowing waterway looked dangerous as always with its roiling water and cargo of speeding logs
and other debris.

I cruised to the marsh, then killed the motor and let
the boat brush up against the reeds and stop. I took out the
binoculars and a pen and notebook and began scanning for
birds. A red-wing blackbird was perched on a reed, and I was
making a note of that sighting when something white flashed
across my peripheral vision. A great American white pelican
was flying low across the grassy expanse. It plopped down
into open water at the far end. I noted it too.

After an hour I started up the motor and turned about to
go home. When I neared the creek entrance I spied turkey
vultures gliding and circling high above the bank. Probably
a dead animal, I thought. Most likely a deer. I would have
turned my attention away if Buddy hadn't stood up, put his
front legs on the bow seat and started barking.

"Knock it off."

Buddy looked back at me, whined once and then only
barked louder, his hindquarters quivering. His persistence
aroused my curiosity, so I passed by the creek and angled
the runabout toward the bank below the vultures, letting the
prow run aground on the sandy shoreline. Something yellow
caught my eye, and Buddy raced to it. He was sniffing it,
his tail hanging low, when I reached him. The yellow was a
blood-stained windbreaker on a man's body, part of which
floated in the coffee-colored water. A pant leg had ridden up
on a sand-covered leg. Because of the bloating, it took me a

moment to realize I was looking at Andre Hadley. His blue jeans were unzipped and pulled down around the middle of his thighs, the flaps swaying in the current. Loose flesh dangled from his mangled groin.

"Whew," I muttered, turning away.

When I looked again I noted the rope knotted around his neck. His face was swollen and gray, which seemed an odd color for a black man.

Andre and I had been talking and laughing only a few days earlier; now he was staring from lifeless eyes. I grabbed Buddy by the collar and pulled him away, back toward the boat, then sat down on a driftwood log. Behind me a patch of pawpaws gave off a foul odor. Like rotten meat.

I dialed 911.

Soon a squad car appeared on the steep, winding lane that led down to the water from Arnaud's restaurant. The lane became nearly impassable in places, dropping off here and there and climbing over embedded boulders, but the car kept bouncing along, stopping only when the pathway petered out into wild grasses at the river's edge.

Murray County Sgt. Rod Shank and Deputy Horace Scroggins got out, crossed the Katy Trail and half-walked, half-slid down the bank to the sandbar. They approached against the backdrop of the towering limestone bluff, which was ribboned with trumpet vine and lined by strata of darker rock.

Tail wagging, Buddy bounded up to the officers.

"Where is he?" Shank asked.

3

When I pointed to Andre's body, I saw now that it had gotten snagged on the roots of a tall cottonwood just back from the river's edge. The tree stood upright as a deacon, as if unwilling to acknowledge what lay at its feet.

"You stay here," Scroggins commanded me. He looked like he was waiting for me to cross him.

Before long, Little Bend's constable, Chuck Cudinhead, showed up.

"Gawd," he wheezed as he bent over to examine it. "That's Andre Hadley, sure enough."

His face showed disgust. He looked away then let out his breath.

"Some animal's been eating at the body."

Two other officers in the county's investigative unit appeared. One started taking photos of the body and the other climbed to the trail, which passed by the bottom of the bluff on its way from Kansas City to St. Louis. Paramedics arrived and brought in a stretcher. The flashing lights of the ambulance cycled through foliage at the river's edge.

Shank walked up to me and planted his boots a couple of feet apart.

"You have any idea how this may have happened, Archer?"

"No …. Hate crime? Sex act that got out of hand?"

"Yeah, I could come up with those ideas myself."

The constable and Scroggins looked on silently. Cudinhead took off his Stetson and scratched his head, which was bald and a bit misshapen, like the top of a badly turned newel post.

Before long, the deputy who had been examining the trail, a bulldog of a man, joined the others.

"There's bike tracks by the trail. The dirt is scuffed up and bushes are broken up. There's footprints all over. A bike could have gone off the bank...the tracks are deep in the mud. They could have been made Sunday morning, after the rain."

"Hadley rode his bike on the trail most mornings," Cudinhead said. "Exercising."

"That's probably what he was doing," Shank said, looking over at the body. He then theorized about the crime—in an elementary way. "Whoever did this probably stopped Hadley on the trail, killed him and threw his body into the water. An attack on the path would likely go unnoticed."

That section of it, just below the country home of Arnaud's owner was heavily wooded and screened by vegetation.

Shank thought a moment. "The killer may have pushed the bike into the river after the body. Let's get divers out to search the river. And get casts made of the footprints." He glanced at the deputy. "Also, organize a search of the area to see if anyone saw anything."

The sergeant looked out over the river and let emotion show for the first time.

"Whoever did this was seriously warped," he spit out before turning to hike back to the squad car.

2

Though few took it that seriously at the time, a foretaste of the violence that ended Andre's life had come six days earlier—at the kickoff for his campaign for Murray County commissioner. I had decided to drop in at that event out of boredom. Not much happens in Little Bend. Ordinarily, that is.

I should have sensed trouble when I noticed the black truck idling outside Andre's apartment, but I didn't. Which would be no surprise to anyone who knows me. I'm laid-back and don't waste my time worrying about run-ins with dangerous men. Trouble mostly finds those who seek it out, in my experience, and I've never looked for it. I've heard it said that you see the world not as it is but as you are. I like to be a nice guy, so I suppose I think everybody else does too. I glanced at the driver, prepared to wave, but he didn't look over.

I had driven over from the river, where I'd been fishing. I ducked my head to walk into the apartment—I'm six-foot-five, so doorways in older houses can be too low, especially when I've got a hat on, and that day I was wearing my fishing hat. What greeted me made me do a double-take. The room's elegance blew me away.

But the high style should have been no surprise. Andre and his partner Charles Parker sold pricey antiques in the store below.

Andre hadn't economized on the food and drink. He'd arrayed hors d'oeuvres on the Chippendale mahogany dining table and an assortment of wines stood sentinel on the gilt-edged sideboard.

Several of the men wore jackets and ties, and everyone, except for me, was dressed for a social occasion. I was wearing camo, as I often did when out of doors. I had a grease mark on my sleeve from when I'd pulled up the boat's motor to check the propeller, and a notebook stuck out of a pocket of my cargo pants.

Sarah—Sarah Jennings Smithson, that is—was welcoming guests.

That was the second shock.

Sarah was attractive, strikingly so, but what defined her in most people's mind was her money. She was a scion of an old banking family, one of the state's wealthiest. I didn't know her then, but, like everyone else in town, I had heard the gossip about her when she arrived from Kansas City. She wasn't able to go anywhere without drawing attention. Her confidence made her stick out, but her clothes did as well. She had designer labels on her T-shirts and jeans.

She had moved here a year ago after her divorce, which many assumed was nasty because of her money and her socialite status. She and her two children were living at the Jennings place. "Farm" was what the family called it, but that was an affectation. The Jenningses had been using the 1,000-plus acre property as a weekend getaway, a hunting preserve and a place to stable their horses.

Sarah was now looking at me with this cool, blank expression.

She walked up.

"This is a campaign event for Andre Hadley."

Her tone put me off. I give people some slack, but I don't much care for snobs.

"Yes. I want to hear what Andre has to say."

Sarah took in her breath and introduced herself, though she looked like she would rather not.

"Jack Archer," I said.

She let her demeanor thaw ever so slightly. Harry Bishop was standing next to her.

"Do you know Harry?"

She made it plain that she directed my attention to Harry less out of good manners than a desire to turn to others more important. But I wasn't interested in how much regard she had for me; her opinion was her business, not mine. Life's too short to worry about what people think about you. Harry was a friend, and he was conservative and didn't fit in with this gathering either. Most of the others, like Margot Laribee—she was the First Christian Church minister—could be counted among the few liberals in town.

It was no mystery why Harry had come. He was worried that a planned industrial hog farm would damage his bed-and-breakfast business. Andre was on record as opposing the farm.

Andre didn't look like your typical politician as he worked the room; he was too trusting, too eager to please. The group was subdued and was no doubt thinking what I was: that he didn't have a prayer.

When Andre got around to me, he was his usual self, boisterous and friendly. He made people feel he liked them. Despite his taste for graceful living, he had the common touch.

"I think you'll appreciate what I have to say," Andre said. "If you want to join my campaign, stop by the store."

"Maybe I will." But I said that only to be sociable.

While we were talking, Sarah glanced at me from across the room and, when she saw me looking back at her, flashed me a tight smile.

Andre said, "Excuse me a minute."

He took a spoon and knocked it against his coffee cup.

"Thank you all for coming here tonight." He spoke in a loud voice. I realized then he knew how to command a room. Maybe he had better prospects than I had believed. "I want to especially thank my campaign manager. I think you all know Charles." He pointed to Charles, who smiled broadly. The two were partners in their personal life as well as their business and planned to marry. That news had spread across the town like a grass fire.

"And also my treasurer, Sarah Smithson," Andre continued. She looked steadily at the candidate, a slight smile acknowledging his introduction. "Sarah has a few words she wants to say. Though she is new to our little town, the way she has fought to preserve this unique area is making her a force here, and I'm happy to be working closely with her."

She tucked a strand of hair behind an ear, tugged down her jacket over her svelte shape and took a deep breath. She was some years older than me, in her mid-30s, I guessed. Standing there, she was beautiful, like a statue.

"I'm so pleased to see you here," she said in a clear voice. "We need to keep our wilderness and farm countryside natural, and that is why we are working hard to stop the hog farm. But that is not enough. We need new leadership to achieve the local government we deserve. We need Andre to win this election to the county commission. Let's all give him a hand to show our appreciation for what he's doing."

When the clapping tapered off, Andre again took the floor.

"I'm running for office because we need an independent voice on the county commission. You've all heard the rumors. You know how our county operates…"

My attention drifted. I thought about the bass I'd caught that afternoon, which had dived below my boat, making reeling him in a challenge. He was no trophy fish but he was good-sized and wily and fought hard for several minutes before I could get him alongside the boat and into my net.

Out on the street, the truck was still there.

"...As you all know, we face an uphill battle," Andre said as I tuned in again. "And not only because of our progressive, reform-minded views. I know that Murray County, unlike much of the rest of the country, may not be ready to elect a black man." Andre smiled knowingly, as did several of his listeners.

More to the point, I thought, this district wasn't likely to elect an openly gay man.

"But with your help, I believe..." Andre continued.

Staccato bursts of semi-automatic rifle fire, followed by the roar of an accelerating vehicle, interrupted the candidate mid-sentence. The room was deathly silent as the alarmed guests looked at one another.

Behind Andre on the floor, on the Persian carpet, I saw shards of glass from the shattered window at his back. I slipped down the stairs, with Harry hustling behind me.

But when we stepped outside, there was nothing to see. Only the streetlights reflecting on the rain-covered street. The truck had disappeared.

Rifle cartridges lay in the gutter.

"He's long gone," I said.

Harry, a fireplug of a man, nodded.

He ran his hand over his flattop. "Andre is sticking his neck out."

When we got back upstairs, Sarah stood next to Andre. Above Andre's head, bullet holes pockmarked the ceiling.

I stopped counting them when I reached seven.

3

The next morning a knock at the door woke me. I tried to ignore it, but the knocking only got louder. I threw off the covers and checked the time on my cell phone.

7:30 a.m. Jeesh.

The arm of a police uniform showed through the window in my front door. When I opened it, Detective Sgt. Shank and Deputy Scroggins stood on my porch. Shank looked muscular and fit and crisply pressed, a contrast to the older, heavy-set and sloppy Scroggins, whom I was familiar with. He'd made a poor impression on me by collaring a drunk with uncalled-for roughness while working security at the restaurant.

"Yes?" I said.

"We want to ask you about the shooting last night at Andre Hadley's home," Shank said.

"I was there, but I can't tell you anything."

"We'll decide that," the sergeant said, looking up at me.

"When we interviewed Hadley he said you and Harry Bishop went down to the street right after the shooting."

"Yes, that's true."

"See anything?"

"Nothing to see. An empty street."

"Did any of the others present act strange?"

"What do you mean?"

"Was anybody nervous? Or not surprised by the shooting?"

"No, I didn't see anything like that. When I arrived, I saw a pickup parked on the street with the engine running. But it was gone when Harry and I went downstairs."

"Can you describe it?"

"It was black with a Missouri plate. Dodge Ram 3500 dually. Four door, with a tool box. It had a dent in the right front fender and a Confederate flag decal on the cab's back window."

Shank was scrutinizing me, not bothering to hide his skepticism. I should have disguised my near-photographic memory. Around Little Bend, being smart makes you weird.

"You saw all that while walking by?"

"Yes."

"You must have studied that truck."

I shrugged.

They asked a few more questions, then I showed them out.

A black Ram truck passed me that afternoon on my way to the bar. I pressed the accelerator on my pickup, thinking I would get the truck's license number. But as I sped up the truck also raced ahead, then veered off onto a gravel side road. I let it go, knowing I couldn't catch it in my old Ford.

Once I got to the restaurant, I phoned Sgt. Shank.

"I spotted a truck on Highway 40 like that parked in front of Andre's last night."

He didn't show much interest.

"Did you get a license number?"

"No."

His response was sarcastic. "Well, that's not very helpful then, is it?"

I hung up. Had he been polite, I would have told him that the driver was a big guy with a shaved head. Like the man in the truck outside Andre's.

At ten the next morning, I bounded up to the side door of Andre's store. If I had known the full extent of what I was entangling myself in, I might have stayed home. But, of course, I didn't.

Anyway, I had decided to volunteer for his campaign. I didn't share Andre's political stance—I lean libertarian, to the extent I have a political persuasion—but the more I thought about the guy shooting up the apartment, the more I was inclined to get involved.

Andre, Sarah and Charles were sitting around an old library table in the back room. Andre jumped up and pulled up an antique kitchen chair.

"Hey. Come in," he said. "Here's the best chair in the house!"

His try at humor didn't make it.

When I told him I wanted to join his campaign, Andre smiled and looked at Charles. "See, not everyone is taking the shooting that seriously."

He turned to me. "Charles thinks I should drop out."

"I don't think it's smart to laugh at danger," Charles said.

Andre laughed. "Nothing will happen to us. Somebody was just trying to scare us."

"I think that's true." Sarah was dressed in a jogging outfit but her hair was neatly brushed and she wore earrings.

I turned to Andre. "Do you know anything more about last night?"

"Not really. Shank said they found 7.62-caliber shell casings on the street. The bullets apparently came from an AK47. Deputies are interviewing neighbors as well as everybody who was in the room, but I think the only information they got so far was what you told them."

I looked down at the table where campaign fliers were arrayed. The four-color sheet displayed a close-up of Andre's face, photos of him talking to citizens and customers, and a picture of him on the river bank. The layout was pleasing. The display and body type were clean and readable on high-grade paper.

"What do you think?" Sarah asked with an amused expression.

"They look smart," I said.

"Can you hand out a dozen of them to your neighbors?" Andre asked.

"I can take more than that. Give me 25." I risked a sidelong glance at Sarah. She was studying the wall.

"Great," Andre said.

The three of them began to talk about raising money.

"Why don't you approach Max?" I suggested. "He has money."

"He's a generous donor," Sarah said.

"Maybe you should make the appeal," I said to her. "He likes women."

She dismissed my idea, evidently aware of Max's reputation as a womanizer.

"No, the candidate should make the contact."

"I agree," Andre said. "I should do it."

I crossed the street and got to work. I'm not one to procrastinate—that only causes stress. Eric Nelson stood behind the General Store's counter when I walked in. He was the athletic type. If I had to guess, I would say he was a running back in college and a frat boy, but not one of the obnoxious sort. Eric was one of the good guys.

I found a bottle of bug repellent on a back shelf and brought it to the front. As Eric was recording the sale, I mentioned the shooting.

He raised an eyebrow. "The police need to put a stop to that."

"Uh huh. I'm supporting Andre. The shooting clinched it for me."

I handed a leaflet to him.

"Would you consider backing him too?"

Eric was the town's mayor, so his endorsement would be a major boost to Andre's candidacy. Eric was conservative but he had an independent streak and the race was non-partisan.

"Some of my customers won't like it but I'll support him." He handed me my change. "I'm not excited about him but he's better than his opponent. Maybe my endorsement will stop this intimidation nonsense. You can use my name. Jane will probably let you use her name too." Jane was his wife. "I'll check with her."

I jogged back across the street and folded myself into the cab of my truck. It had a crease in a rear panel and its red paint was faded, but the engine started up smoothly as always. Thinking there might be chatter about the previous night's shooting, I took out my phone and punched the app that monitors police communications. I like to keep up on what's happening. But on this afternoon there was nothing; only a domestic situation and a break-in at a backyard shed.

As I drove to my next stops, I relaxed and took in the

countryside. Around a town like this one the scenery is a world apart from a suburban street. That's the way I like it. I much prefer nature's disorder to man's planned arrangements. Shrubs and small trees crowded the edge of the narrow blacktop, which led to my place, a 20-acre truck farm I had let go wild. That made upkeep easy. As I reached it and passed by, I surveyed my stand of pin oaks, which still held some russet leaves.

I continued on to my neighbors to the north. A watchful stone deer stood in their yard, which had been denuded of all vegetation except for grass. Landscaping wasn't one of Vern Barlow's interests. To one side of the Barlows' house a barn that had once been white perched on a rise. Several part-Angus steers waded ankle-deep in manure in the attached pen. Tufts of cattle hair clung to the pen's barbed-wire fence, which sagged in places where the steers had been leaning against it to reach the longer grass growing on the other side.

My pickup lurched as I slowly navigated the washed-out driveway. A black mongrel dog strained on its chain and began to bark.

Vern was in the machine shed, working on his tractor. The smell of oil and gasoline hung heavy in the air.

"Cool day." I sounded like a farmer.

"Sure is," Vern answered, wiping his hands on his Levis.

I went through my campaign pitch.

"I'm not voting for that guy."

"Why not?"

Vern paused. He looked like he shouldn't have to explain.

"He's not one of us. He's marrying a man, you know," he said, smirking. "You shouldn't be voting for him either."

With that, Vern clammed up and returned to working on his tractor.

I myself didn't care about anyone's sexual orientation—or whether they got married. I thought that wasn't any of my business. Nevertheless, I told Vern, "I respect your opinion." Then I felt disgusted with myself for my phoniness.

Vern ignored my effort to continue the conversation, however.

"Here's a flier," I said.

Vern continued to work on the tractor. I put the leaflet down on the tractor's tire before leaving.

The dog was still barking.

I drove to the Schultzes. But I got no better results there.

Claud Koster operated a gun-repair business at his home a mile from town. He was an unlikely supporter for Andre, but his place wasn't far out of my way so I stopped in. He nodded, recognizing me as a customer—he'd repaired the firing pin on my shotgun.

When I told him I was working for Andre's campaign, he scowled.

"You can just as well leave."

I tried again to make my points.

He reached down and pulled up a rifle and laid it on the counter.

"I'm not going to tell you again."

4

Andre stood by the antiques store counter the next morning—a Saturday—going through estate jewelry.

"Looking for a ring?" I asked.

"Yes," he said, beaming.

"Planning a large wedding?"

"Just a few friends. In St. Louis." St. Louis was the only Missouri city allowing gay marriage.

"Are there any leads in the shooting?"

"The detective questioned Koster. He drives a black truck and everyone knows about his opioid habit."

"I wouldn't put the shooting past Claud. But the truck outside your store wasn't Claud's."

"How do you know?"

"Claud's has only two doors. I got a look at it yesterday when I stopped at his place."

"Is he going to vote for me?" Andre asked with a smirk.

"Not a chance. I didn't find anyone excited about your

campaign, if you want to know the truth.

"The mayor will endorse you, however." That brought a big smile to his face.

"Really. That's huge. I'll talk to him. Maybe he'll have some advice for me."

Andre pushed his way through the restaurant's double doors later that day. He caught my eye (I was tending bar) then walked over to Max Arnaud, who was sitting on his favorite stool at the bar's end, where he liked to pass the time with his pals.

But on this afternoon the restaurant owner was alone with a drink in front of him.

"Mind if I sit down?"

Max nodded toward the next stool. Then he signaled me.

Andre shot me a conspiratorial glance as I waited for his order.

"A Blue Moon."

He turned to Max. "I imagine you heard I'm running for county commission. I know you're a pillar of this town, and I'd like to have your support."

Max a pillar of the community? That's over the top.

Max didn't say anything at first. He just stared at Andre, until he became uncomfortable. Andre cleared his throat and began to talk about his reform platform.

"Well, I think you're right about what needs to be done,"

Max interrupted. "But you're tilting at windmills. Nothing will change. I'll endorse you though."

"If you could make a contribution to my campaign, that would be much appreciated too."

Max was quiet for a moment. "No. I've given you all the money I'm going to give you."

Andre was taken back. "What do you mean? You've never given me money."

"I guess your mom didn't tell you. I've supported the two of you."

"What?"

"You heard me." Max got up.

Andre looked dumbfounded. He took a gulp of his beer.

"You better explain," he said as he also stood.

"Ask your mom."

"I'm asking you." Andre's tone was angry.

"Ask your mom. I have to go."

Max waddled away in the direction of his office. A portly man, his womanizing was remarkable. He looked like the guy in high school who could never get a date, except that he was middle-aged now.

Andre took another swallow of his beer. His hands were trembling. Then he walked out, agitation showing in every move he made.

5

That Sunday I tried to forget the shooting and my gnaw-ing apprehension about it. Thinking about something too much will do that to you. I did my laundry and posted some photos to Instagram. Then I got out of the house and worked on my latest canoe. I had built a racing canoe of my own design for the annual marathon race on the Missouri from Kansas City to St. Louis, and when another competitor want -ed one too, I made a second one and sold it to him. That was the beginning of another of my income-producing enterprises.

That afternoon, I put away my tools and went to a party at the home of Angelica Sanchez, a server at Arnaud's. When I arrived, a dozen or so other Mizzou fans were watching the game that would decide whether Missouri would make it into the Final Four. Max was there too. He and Angelica had been hanging out together for a couple of months.

I started chatting with an MU grad student. She had a dry

wit. But my interest wasn't reciprocated, and I headed off to home alone.

On Monday morning I stopped at the police station to see if there were any developments. The station was in a narrow, old stone building with a vacant second story whose windows were obscured by dust and cobwebs. Constable Cudinhead sat at his desk looking like he was auditioning for the role of Southern sheriff in a movie. He was in uniform, his Stetson pushed back on his head, and he was tipped back in his wooden chair, cleaning his fingernails with a pocketknife.

I had an urge to mimic him but stifled it. Antagonizing constables is a low-percentage sport.

Cudinhead set the chair down, closed the knife and looked at me with a face devoid of friendliness.

"What can I do for you?" He looked out the window as if he had better things to do than talk to me.

"You know anything more about who shot up Andre's apartment?"

"The sheriff's handling that."

"Yes, I know. But I thought you might have heard something."

He didn't respond.

"Well, thanks for the information." But I knew my irony would be lost on him.

"Don't let the door hit you on the way out," he said without looking up.

The constable's rudeness left a sour taste, but its insignificance was soon put into context.

For the next morning, Tuesday, I found Andre's body.

The following morning I was grappling with the viciousness of his slaying. The killer's cruelty had invaded my mind and exploded my sense of what was normal. I needed to talk about it. About nine o'clock I drove into town.

When I got there, Sarah was having breakfast with her children at one of the wrought-iron tables outside the General Store. That reminded me this was spring break. Though reserved, Sarah greeted me with the hint of a smile—one that didn't quite connect. I had intended to be aloof when I saw her again but found myself returning her smile.

While I stood there, trying to think what to say, she relieved the tension by asking me to sit down. It was a sublime experience to be next to her—I was certain she knew most men felt that way in her presence.

"What a glorious morning!" she said after a moment.

She plainly didn't know about Andre, and I wasn't in a hurry to tell her. I don't enjoy being the bearer of bad news.

I glanced around the town. Across the street Tom Sanders, editor of the weekly *Murray County Trader,* was setting out more copies of the current edition in a rack in front of his newspaper office, which occupied a building that had once been an automotive garage. The town of 794 souls looked peaceful and safe.

But, of course, Andre's death had put the lie to that. I steeled myself.

"You must not have heard about Andre," I said.

"What about him?"

"He was murdered."

"What!"

"I found his body yesterday along the river."

I thought she looked at me suspiciously, but only for a moment. I had wondered whether Andre was one of her liberal projects, rather than a genuine friend, but her anguish answered that question. She turned to her children, who were squabbling over a cinnamon roll and weren't paying us any attention. "That's my roll. You give it back," her daughter was saying, with her chin thrust forward. She was a couple of years younger than her brother, who I now know was nine.

"George," Sarah said sharply. "Take Emily into the store and buy some candy." She reached into her purse, took out a couple of dollars and handed them to her son. When the two had happily run into the store, she turned back to me.

"How...was he killed?"

I told her what I knew, without being graphic.

"My God!" She dropped her head into her hands, then looked up. "I should never have encouraged him to seek office."

Blaming the death on herself made no sense.

"He wanted to run. And we don't know why he was

killed."

She didn't respond.

"Poor Charles. He must be heartbroken! They were to be married next week." She had been helping them prepare for the wedding. She looked over at the antiques store. "I'm going over to see him. You come too. He needs support. Jane will watch the kids."

Charles must have seen us on our way because he stood in the doorway, his plump body filling it. He'd been crying and made no effort to mask his grief.

"I'm so sorry, Charles," Sarah said, hugging him.

She followed him through the store's back room, as we made our way around stacks of old dishware and kitchen furnishings. Linens filled cupboards and pots hung from the ceiling. We went into the front room, and Charles lowered himself into an antique rocker while Sarah and I sat in a pair of Regency wing chairs.

"I don't know what I'm going to do!" Charles said, his voice breaking. "He meant everything to me. We had all these plans—for the wedding, our honeymoon, for our future."

Several clocks chimed on the hour.

"Can I do anything for you?" Sarah asked.

"Not right now." He wiped his eyes with his pudgy fingers.

He relapsed into silence, then burst out: "The police asked if I had any idea who may have killed Andre. Isn't it fucking obvious? I'm sure it was one of these god-awful homophobes! Maybe that white supremacist minister, Hunthausen, or one of his cult!"

Sarah put a hand on his arm. "Try not to get worked up. That won't help."

Charles let his rage subside.

"They asked if Andre or I knew anyone capable of committing such a crime," he said soberly. "Why don't they consider the obvious? Somebody did not want a gay, black man sitting on the county commission. Especially not one who wanted to reform it."

He paused. "Or maybe someone hated that Andre and I were getting married."

Then he told Sarah he and Andre had quarreled Saturday night.

"Andre got mad and stormed out of the house when I demanded he drop out of the campaign. I just didn't want him to get hurt. That guy with the gun was still out there.... It's my fault he ran out...."

He roused himself. "But I was right. The guy was out there...waiting for him....

"I can't stand it that we lost each other at a time when we were angry with each other. We usually got along so well. It is just too much to bear....

"I'm now afraid too."

"I don't think you're in danger," Sarah said. "The police will be on alert."

He sighed.

The three of us walked to the back door.

"He may be in trouble," she said cryptically after Charles

closed the door behind us. "But not for the reason he thinks."

6

"Hey, is anybody alive in here?"

The voice boomed as if from a loudspeaker.

"What does a guy have to do to get a drink?"

I struck the final note in "Laura" and held it for the full count. As a rule Arnaud's customers enjoyed my playing. The jazz created a pleasant atmosphere for dining. But this guy was an exception. I stood up from the piano and looked over to see who had walked in, even though it was still a couple of minutes until our weekday opening time of five o'clock.

He was a regular, a guy who sold ads for a country music radio station in Boonville. He looked haggard in his rumpled brown slacks and green-patterned shirt.

"Hey, Ted." The acrid smell of smoke from his cigarette stung my nose. "What'll you have? The usual?"

"Yeah." He rubbed his receding hairline with one hand and held his cigarette with the other.

I took down the Jack Daniels whiskey and filled a jigger.

"You're not like most bartenders."

I shrugged. "You're like most salesmen."

That was snarky, but it had the desired effect of shutting him up.

He was right, however.

I was an unlikely worker in the hospitality industry. I'm not anti-social but making small talk isn't easy for me. Maybe Max hired me because he thought my size would discourage rowdiness. Or he may just have been a good guy.

But anyway, the job had worked out well. Max set a high bar, no pun intended, for the restaurant's food and drink, to the point where he sometimes was so demanding that he had trouble keeping his help. But I didn't mind his exacting standards, which had inspired me to become a decent bartender. I even developed a couple of craft cocktails that became popular with our customers.

The bottom line, of course, was that I had needed the job. I had to have a paycheck to make ends meet.

Most kids who grew up in Little Bend couldn't wait to move to a big city. Not me. I had lived in St. Louis during college but became depressed by the crowds, the traffic, the endless concrete, the lack of wild places. I preferred this town where everyone is friendly. In Little Bend I was comfortable and could be myself.

I brought Ted his change. "Heard from Mildred?"

The salesman's wife had left him two weeks earlier. He shook his head.

I didn't expect his bleak mood to lift, so I settled my

frame against the liquor cabinet and turned to my own thoughts. It was still too early for the dinner customers who would soon fill the restaurant, known for its gourmet food as well as its bluff-top view of the Missouri.

When Charles entered the restaurant, he came in quietly and looked around, blinking in the low light, then shuffled to the bar.

I walked over to him while drying a glass. He looked miserable sitting on the bar stool. Shapeless and bent over, like a big manatee. When he glanced up at me, his eyes were bloodshot.

"You doing okay?"

He shrugged without looking up. He said neighbors and friends had been bringing food to the house and had come by to check up on him.

"I'm swimming in food."

Then, in a low voice, he asked: "You found him, didn't you?"

I nodded. Down the bar Ted was staring into his Jack and Coke.

"The police told me the horrible things that were done to him…. The deputies were crude! Disgusting! Especially that guy Scroggins. They took me to the sheriff's department, harassed me every chance they got. Then the sergeant badgered me about our sex lives. Asked if we were into S&M. The bastard! He can't imagine I'm a victim too."

I remembered what Sarah said about his being in trouble. I didn't know what to say. His angry expression collapsed.

"They think Andre may have died from drowning rather than suffocation. I hate to think of him in the water. If he was alive when he was in the river, he would have panicked. He couldn't swim. And he was already so terribly injured."

A re-run of the final minutes of the game that advanced Mizzou to the Final Four, the one I'd cheered at Angelica's, was showing on the flat-screen TV behind the bar. Ted was watching it.

I remembered Charles was fond of Negronis, and he was ready for one. I was looking in the refrigerator for an orange wheel for the garnish when the two brothers charged in, talking loudly and laughing. They operated a farm implement dealership in Paradise.

"Two drafts," the older brother, a beefy guy, said, straddling a bar stool and pushing his John Deere cap back on his head. I interrupted the drink I was making and brought them their beers.

The big guy looked down the bar at Charles and scrutinized him in the dim light.

"Look who's here. The faggot!"

They laughed.

The salesman looked over and laughed too.

I put Charles' drink down in front of him and walked down the bar to the brothers.

"At least he gets laid," I said, looking the older brother in the eye. I picked up their glasses.

"Get out. We don't need your business."

Neither of them moved. The big guy's face darkened and

he gave me a steely look. "We'll go, but Max will hear about this. Don't think you're getting away with it."

I watched them walk away.

Good luck with that. Tough guys don't impress Max either.

Charles silently nursed his cocktail. When his glass was empty, I brought him a second. Then I left him alone. He stayed at the bar until closing time.

7

Sarah phoned the next morning. She didn't bother with preliminaries.

"Charles has been arrested in Andre's death."

"As you anticipated," I said grimly.

Events were going from bad to worse in a hurry.

"He's in a dither. First his partner is slain and now this. I don't know yet what they're basing their suspicions on, but Shank says murder charges are likely. I've agreed to represent Charles. That's why I phoned you. Assuming charges are filed, I'll need an investigator. I want to hire you."

Coming out of the blue as it did, her offer left me nonplussed.

"I'm not a detective."

"That doesn't matter. I need someone smart like you. But, most of all, I need a native, someone who knows Little Bend's secrets."

I found her flattery annoying—I don't like to be played—

but her argument made sense. I knew the town like my own bedroom, from the Baptist Church bell tower where teens made out to the police station cellar where the constable stashed his bottle of bourbon.

"You can do it in your off hours. I'll pay you well."

I held back, thinking. I was motivated to see Andre's murder solved and Charles exonerated. I couldn't believe he could commit murder. Maybe my initiative would make up for a lack of experience. The challenge was like a magnet.

The bottom line was: I could use the money.

"When do I start?"

"How about this afternoon? I've got to see Charles at the jail. Why don't you come along and listen in?"

"Okay."

"Meet me at the county jail at two."

The county government complex was about 20 minutes from Little Bend, in Marseille (pronounced Mar-*sell*), one of several towns in the region that had French names although their pronunciations were Americanized. The area was once French territory, but Marseille didn't appear to have any French influences. It was a typical Midwestern town with a population of just over 3,000. The county offices and courthouse occupied a modern brick building at the front of a treeless lot, and the sheriff's office and jail complex lay to the rear. Not seeing Sarah's car, I parked and took out my phone. I was scanning an article on President Obama and gun control when Sarah drove up in her Volvo Cross-Country.

"We'll see Bill Henry first," she said.

The county prosecutor was talking to his secretary in his office's antechamber when Sarah approached him.

"Do you have a moment, Bill?"

He nodded, opened his door then followed us into his office.

"Bill, this is Jack Archer." She waved an arm in my direction. "He's doing investigative work for me. I'm representing Charles Parker. I understand you are intending to charge him with the murder of Andre Hadley?"

"Looks like it."

The prosecutor, a small, dapper man with salt-and-pepper hair and black-rimmed glasses, sat on the edge of his desk.

"He's our most likely suspect. So far, the evidence is circumstantial. Trail mud on his tennis shoes, that sort of thing. But neighbors heard them arguing loudly on the day before the death. The argument may have been over finances —his store hasn't been doing too well. Or jealousy may have played a role. An old friend, another dancer, Kyle Hyde, visited Andre earlier in the week. We believe they are, or were, lovers."

He gave her a shrewd look. "There's another thing, rather distasteful, but we can't rule it out. The condition of the body suggests that the death could be due to a sex game that got out of control."

"Oh, God, you can't believe that!"

He looked down. I concluded Sarah said that to try to influence him.

As we walked off toward the jail, she said: "We're lucky Bill's the prosecutor. I wonder about his judgment sometimes, but he plays it straight."

Inside the jail's concrete-block entry Hal Weaver, the presiding county commissioner, was talking to his son Darrell, the police dispatcher. Interesting how relatives got hired for most government jobs around there. Darrell wanted to move up—he was running for county sheriff. Most everyone thought that if he got elected it would only be because of his dad. Most of Darrell's experience was in partying. Sarah greeted them but kept walking.

A deputy led us to Charles' cell. Charles' face brightened at the sight of Sarah. The jail's orange jumpsuit made him appear even more roly-poly than usual.

"Thanks for coming!" he said emotionally.

"How are you doing?" Sarah asked. "Are you comfortable?"

"Comfortable? I don't feel safe. It's crazy in here! Can you get me out?"

"Not today, but soon I hope."

His face turned angry. "I asked if I could go to the funeral on Sunday, but they won't let me! They're heartless."

"I'll talk to the prosecutor to see if he'll have them take you to the funeral." She looked at me, with an expression that said that would never happen. "But now we need to talk about how to defend you and get you out of jail. For that I'll need your help."

She explained that the best defense would be either a credible alibi or evidence that someone else was the killer.

"Are you sure Andre hadn't become involved with someone dangerous?"

"Yes. He was smarter than that."

"Think carefully. Can you tell me anything that might be helpful? Something out of character? An old problem that may have resurfaced?"

Charles thought for a moment. Sarah prodded him.

"Had Andre had a confrontation with anyone? Did he have any enemies?"

"He angered Russ Collins by opposing his hog farm. I told him he should think twice about crossing that guy. But you know Andre. If he thought he was right he stuck to his position. He didn't know the meaning of discretion." He paused a moment. "He also hinted darkly that he knew something else about Russ, something he wouldn't want out."

"That could be important. Do you know what he was talking about?"

"No idea. He refused to say more."

Charles sighed.

"Another thing. Andre approached Max on Saturday about a campaign contribution. When he came home he was disturbed. He wouldn't tell me why. He was in a state. I asked him several times what was wrong, but he just kept telling me it was none of my business."

"I can tell you about that." I related what I'd overheard at the bar.

The revelation baffled Charles.

"Could Max and Andre's mother have been lovers?" I asked. "Max likes women. Overly much, you could say."

Charles looked doubtful.

"Could Max be Andre's father?" Sarah asked.

"Andre's dad left the family when Andre was a toddler, but I met him once," Charles said. "He looked like Andre."

"Even ruling out paternity," Sarah said, "the two might have had a liaison that could have led to a long-term friendship. Or blackmail. But all this is speculation. We don't know that Max actually gave the Hadleys any money. I'll talk to Max and see what I can learn."

Sarah told Charles the prosecutor thought a sex game might be the cause of the death.

"I knew from the questions they were going there," he said. "That detective has it out for me."

"He has to consider all possibilities," Sarah replied.

She asked Charles about the prosecutor's other suspicions. Charles admitted the store wasn't doing well but said money wasn't an issue for the two of them. He denied being jealous.

"Andre and Kyle were old friends. Nothing more."

"If you get charged, I'll want to talk to Kyle. Where'd you go after the fight? Someone must have seen you. Someone must be able to provide you with an alibi."

"I don't think so. I drove around for a while, just to get away. I was distraught, for God's sake. Then I drove to St. Louis, and, when the arboretum opened, sat there on a bench until noon."

Sarah probed further into the quarrel. It had snowballed like so many domestic confrontations do. When Andre wouldn't agree to drop out of the race, Charles had accused him of having delusions of grandeur and things got nasty with lots of name-calling and memories of past wounds.

"I was concerned about Andre's safety, but otherwise I wasn't too upset that he'd walked out," Charles said. "He'd done that before. It wasn't until I went out to the garage Sunday afternoon and saw his bike gone that I got scared. If he'd gone off on his bike, he should have been back by then. I called the police, and they said they'd keep an eye out for him."

"You should have called me," Sarah said. "I could have helped you with the police."

"I was embarrassed about the fight…but, of course, by that time it was too late."

Sarah got back to the point. "If someone overheard the fight, do you think they might have concluded you were angry enough to become violent?"

"People will think anything. But, yeah, I suppose they might think that."

"Well, even a furious quarrel does not prove murder. The prosecution needs proof."

After reassuring Charles she'd return soon, Sarah called

the deputy and we left the cell. "I am worried about what neighbors overheard," she said as we walked down the hall.

"Oh, one other thing. The hog farm hearing is tomorrow. I want you to attend. From what Charles said, we should consider Russ a suspect in Andre's death."

8

The sky was overcast and a drizzle was coming down the next morning as I trotted up the lane to grab the *Murray County Trader* from the mailbox. When I was back in the house and had shaken off the raindrops, I looked at the headline in the top right corner, which read, "Entertainer Found Dead on River Bank." I scanned the article even though the edition had been printed before Charles' arrest. Deadlines are relaxed in small-town journalism.

> *Murray County Commission candidate Andre Hadley was discovered dead Tuesday in the water along the east bank of the Missouri River, north of Interstate 70.*
>
> *Police said the body of Hadley, 35, of Little Bend, had suffered injuries.*
>
> *"We're classifying it as a homicide," said Murray County Detective Sgt. Rod Shank.*
>
> *A boater found the body, he said. Death may have*

occurred several days earlier.

"We're continuing to investigate," Shank said.

I put down the paper and ground some coffee beans, releasing their savory scent. Through the window over the kitchen sink—an ancient model with chipped enamel—I could see a pair of cardinals darting in the tulip tree, which was starting to bloom. Buddy was lying on the stoop looking over the back field, protected from the rain by the overhanging porch roof.

When the coffee began to percolate, I returned to the newspaper, with my cat Dusty brushing against my legs.

Hadley was well known for his performances with the summer stock troupe at the Actor's Theatre in Arrow Rock. He also was co-owner of Artful Antiques, a Little Bend antiques store.

Before moving to Little Bend six years ago, Hadley acted, sang and danced in several professional theaters in St. Louis.

"He was a fine actor and an exceptional dancer," said Kelly Morgan, director of the theater company. "The troupe is poorer for losing him.

"He also was a delightful man with an impish sense of humor. He had many friends in this community and will be missed."

Hadley had recently announced as a candidate for the Murray County Commission, running on a platform that included opposition to the proposed corporate hog farm northwest of Little Bend.

Shank said that the Little Bend Police Department was aiding in the investigation of the death.

Memorial services are set for 2 p.m. Sunday at First Christian Church in Little Bend.

I fixed myself a country breakfast: half a grapefruit, scrambled eggs, toast and a slice of ham When I finished, I put the dirty dishes in a plastic tub in the sink without washing them and left for the hearing.

It was being held in the commission chambers. I say "chambers" advisedly, because the commission met in a long, multi-purpose room. A divider, which was pushed to the sides that morning, allowed the space to be reconfigured as two rooms. When I arrived the commissioners were sitting behind two tables placed end to end. In front of them were a half dozen long rows of folding chairs.

The room was packed.

Russ was huddled with men in suits, representatives of FARMCO, the corporation that had contracted to buy the pork, I soon learned.

Sarah came up to me. "Are camouflage clothes all you own?"

I didn't dignify her question with a reply.

Russ's attorney opened the hearing by making the case that the project would be a boon for the local economy.

"You know, I'm just a farm boy at heart," he said as he wrapped up. "Someday my family and I may move out here and join you in this beautiful setting and benefit from the economic boost you all are going to get from corporate farming. One thing I'm certain of is this farm will be good for the community. Thank you all for listening."

Before sitting down, he passed out brochures displaying photos of spotless buildings, wholesome-looking farm workers and prime hog stock. Anyone from Murray County knew no farm looked like that.

I saw Russ glance over at Sarah. He looked confident.

When she took the podium to respond, she identified herself as a representative of the grassroots group she organized, the Citizens to Preserve Our Countryside. She held up petitions with the names of more than 700 people opposed to the project.

"That's a lot of people. At this point, we probably still outnumber the hog population of Murray County." Laughter rippled through the crowd.

She argued that any advantages of the farm would be outweighed by its negative impact on the county's tourism business and pristine countryside. She also put a picture of a hog waste lagoon up on the video screen and said the stench from the lagoons would drift for miles. She stressed that the pesticides and antibiotics used by factory farms to reduce disease would end up in the wastes, and those substances could spread in the soil and water and cause health problems.

The crowd was still, listening intently. Russ had a guarded expression. With a hint of menace.

Sarah put up a photo of a pregnant sow in a gestation pen too small to allow it to turn around.

"This is animal abuse. That alone should stop you from approving this project."

Sounds too arrogant, I thought. Appeals to their better nature weren't going to work with these commissioners.

Then she went a step further.

"If you approve this farm, you can be sure the people who signed this petition will be joined at election time by hundreds of others who will see that this is your last vote to discount their welfare."

The crowd erupted in applause.

Russ' attorney responded that the farm would provide a good living for its employees, most of whom would live in the county.

"That's not true!" a woman shouted from the audience. A susurrus of agreement came from a smattering of citizens.

At that point, Hal Weaver took the microphone and asserted control. "If there are any more outbursts, the disruptive individuals will be escorted from the room," the presiding commissioner said in his distinctive slow drawl. He then allowed other speakers, including a member of End Animal Abuse, who offered undercover photos of mistreatment of animals at FARMCO operations. But Weaver cut him short.

"You can leave the photos on that table." His tone indicated the man's testimony was over. "Anyone else want to speak?"

The hearing stretched out for another hour, the temperature in the room rising with the emotional heat as tempers flared. Hal announced that the commission would vote after a recess.

When the vote came, only Darlene Spencer, the commission's sole woman, opposed the project. I could see Sarah's shoulders slump. But she looked as resolute as ever as she walked out.

I met up with her in the hall.

"I shouldn't have brought up the animal cruelty issue." She said that as much to herself as me. "I let passion override my common sense."

"Those places are callous to animals, "I said. "But it may not have been smart to threaten the commissioners."

She frowned at me before stalking off.

It was past noon, so I drove to Marge's Country Café, where I could get good comfort food. I took a seat in a booth by the window. Outside the glass lay a pothole-pocked blacktop street and, beyond that, a silent and neglected trailer park, a bleak scene that reflected my mood.

I'd just begun eating my meatloaf when I realized that I wasn't the only person at the hearing who had retreated to that down-home place. Across the room Hal sat alone hunched over a table, with his long, thin hands encircling a coffee cup. I watched him, curious, in part because he was a neighbor with whom I had only a nodding acquaintance. His large stone house, castle-like with its turreted towers, sat on a 10-acre lot upriver from my property. His home looked out of place in an area with few upscale houses.

Soon Russ stepped through the front door. Hal glanced over at him then looked down again at the table. The developer surveyed the room then joined Hal. A waitress came for Russ' order. The men talked in low tones.

I kept my eye on them. When they finished eating, Russ took an envelope from his jacket pocket and set it on the table.

Hal picked it up.

Then Russ stood up, a cynical grin on his face. He said something more and left. I watched through the window as he walked out to his truck. A burly guy sat in the passenger seat, his elbow extending out the open window.

I stayed at the café until Hal put money on the table for the bill and walked out as well.

I phoned Sarah to tell her about the exchange but got no answer.

9

An incident that evening at the region's annual cancer fundraiser darkened the shadow of suspicion falling on Russ. I was tending bar as a volunteer—Max had recruited me for the role after donating the food and liquor and the use of his restaurant. The guests were the society of Little Dixie, a label a dozen counties along the Missouri had acquired because of the tobacco and hemp plantations that once thrived there and the Southern flavor of the area's early culture. The region had more slaves than anywhere else in the state and sympathized with the South during the Civil War.

The event offered an insider's view of the local culture. As the guests strolled in, men were seeking out other men to talk business or sports, and their wives were all smiles and friendliness as they scrutinized one another's appearances. The invitations for the gala, Springtime on the River, suggested Western wear, and some men and women were wearing jeans and cowboy boots.

Sarah arrived and was quickly surrounded by a knot of women. I knew they envied her status as a Jennings, a family that remained socially prominent not only because of its wealth but because it had been one of Missouri's leading pioneer families. She was smiling with restraint as she chatted with those courting her.

She and the other guests began looking through the silent auction items and then drifted over to the dining tables.

I rested my elbows on the bar top, taking in the scene, as the professional pianist, the only black person in the room, tapped out the notes to "Sentimental Journey" with long, elegant fingers.

Then I mixed up more Pink Lady cocktails, the gala's signature drink. While everyone was dining, I took out my copy of *Riding the Rap,* which I was re-reading because of my sudden interest in detective work. Elmore Leonard wrote dialogue few writers could match.

Angelica, who was serving, interrupted my reading on her way to the kitchen.

"Drinking the supplies?" I'd poured myself some scotch.

I smiled. "Mind your own business."

Max walked up.

"You look enchanting tonight!" He leaned into Angelica. "How about taking off early?"

"You decide when my shift ends." She gave him a smile.

Max glanced at his wife, Tina, who sat alone at their table. A blonde with delicate features, she looked attractive but embittered. She'd been drinking too much.

Max turned to me. "Make me another."

I was mixing the drink when I overheard Eric say in a loud voice: "You don't give a damn about this town."

I glanced over at his table. He was talking to Russ, who was standing in the aisle.

"You may be mayor, but you're still nobody here," Russ replied.

The word about Eric's endorsement of Andre must have gotten around. Russ' face was red with fury and he slurred his words, showing the effects of too much bourbon.

"You outsiders are trouble. We don't want you here!"

He pointed a finger in Eric's face. "Why don't you sell that worthless store and get out of here?"

Eric responded forcefully. "I think you owe me an apology."

"That's not going to happen!"

For a moment it looked as if the standoff would erupt into violence.

Then with a contemptuous look, Eric turned his back on Russ.

Sarah and several other women gathered around Jane. Soon they moved to the bar, and one of them said: "A vodka martini for Jane. She needs one!"

I started making it up. Several of the women looked at me with interest. "Who is he?" one whispered.

Sarah stood across the bar from me. She was drawing the eye of many of the men in the room, and she had my undivided attention as well. She wore snug jeans, and her pinned-up hair and the open collar on her western-style blouse exposed her luminous skin.

I concentrated on filling the orders from the women.

"I don't know why there's so much fuss about a hog farm," one woman said.

"What an interesting point of view," Sarah said dryly, looking over at me and giving me a restrained—and slightly crooked—smile.

10

That night I slept fitfully. Russ' florid face appeared in a nightmare, then receded behind Max's leering grin. The face transmogrified once more, into Andre's glassy eyes, gray skin and gaping mouth. When I awoke with a start, the room was dark. I couldn't get back to sleep, and I was still tossing and turning when the first light of dawn began filtering through the window.

I mulled over the murder, and thought again that I knew nothing about tracking down a killer.

Until my father's death I had lived a sheltered life in fact, though everything changed then. I found myself alone in a cold world when my mother ran away with a boyfriend while I was a senior in high school. She had been lonely and depressed ever since my stepfather, a kind man who worked as an administrator at the University of Missouri, died two years earlier. The abandonment prepared me to understand the rage of mistreated teen-agers. But this case didn't involve a mixed-up youth.

I would have to extemporize, learning as I went. My thoughts returned to the murder.

The rope knotted around Andre's neck could have been used to cause asphyxiation and enhance an orgasm during a sex game, but it would have had to go wildly awry to end with Andre's castration.

And if the rope wasn't part of a sex act, but instead the instrument of a hate crime, why wasn't it tied in a noose, as in most lynchings? That would have made the killing easier. I'd read somewhere that killing a person isn't as easy as most people think.

I got up, washed up and grabbed a bowl of cereal and an orange. Then I went outside and called Buddy.

"Let's make a food run? What do you say?"

Buddy shaped himself into a wriggling coil. I put on a felt hat for protection from the rain, pulled it down at what I imagined was a rakish angle, and walked out to my truck, signaling to Buddy to jump into the truck bed.

The feed store, covered in weathered plywood panels with a few flecks of old green paint, sat just west of Main Street. Inside there was the musty smell of grain and a faded Funk's Hybrid Seed Corn advertisement tacked to a wall. The place was right out of the 1950s. The constable rested his ample bulk against a stack of feed, and the store's owner worked at the counter. Across from him, paying for a sack of oats, stood Sarah. She was dressed again in jeans but now also wore a jeans jacket.

She turned around and looked at me. "Did you enjoy the party?"

"That might be going too far. By the way, I need to talk to you...."

But before I could say more the front door opened and banged against the wall. Billy Hatcher, a wiry man with a ponytail and a handlebar mustache, slouched in and looked us over. With his sullen but aggressive expression, he could have been an actor in a spaghetti western.

He turned to me and I noted open sores on his face. "What kind of dog is that?" He smelled of manure and BO. He was talking about Buddy.

"He's a Catahoula mix."

Saying nothing more, Billy picked up a 40-pound bag of dog food and took it to the counter. The others remained silent while he paid for it and left.

"At least he feeds his dogs." The constable sneered. "I wouldn't have bet on that."

It was no secret that Billy ran a dog-fighting operation. It was illegal but the police looked the other way. They had jailed Billy more than once, however, on other charges, from driving under the influence to marijuana use.

I changed the topic to the murder investigation.

"Did the divers find Andre's bike?"

"Nope. Shank said they went as far down as the interstate."

"It wouldn't have drifted that far. It would have hung up

on the underwater tree stumps."

"I suppose you know what you're talking about," the constable said.

"They did find a witness," he volunteered. "Ralph Moon. The odd guy who lives in the trailer down from the Arnauds. He said a black dog attacked a guy on a bike and another man was there. Ralph then got scared and ran away."

Cudinhead then pointed to his head, indicating that he thought Ralph was mentally unreliable.

"Does the sergeant now have another suspect in mind? Someone besides Charles?"

"Beats me. They aren't taking what Ralph said seriously."

After buying a sack of dog food, I asked Sarah to step outside with me. I told her about the meeting of Hal and Russ at the café.

"That's intriguing," she said thoughtfully.

She told me the police were making progress in their investigation. "Shank and his investigators have done some good work. They wanted to find out where Andre went after he left home, and Shank had a hunch he most likely stayed overnight with a friend. So they began interviewing his friends. They hit pay dirt when they talked to Kelly Morgan. She admitted Andre slept over at her house."

"Hmm."

"The two of them stayed up late talking. Kelly tried to persuade Andre to make up with Charles, but he wouldn't do it. He left her the next morning, saying he was going for his daily ride."

"I suppose we should interview Kelly too."

"Yes. Do that next week."

At that we parted. Her preemptory commands rankled a bit, though I knew they shouldn't have—she was my employer.

I tossed the dog food into the truck bed and drove around the corner to the General Store. Unpainted shelves lined the walls, and in the rear, past the canned goods, the garden supplies and the hardware section, coveralls and other clothing were laid out. I picked out a pair of work gloves.

"Russ is a bully," I told Eric as I put the gloves on the counter. "Ignore him. We appreciate your store. If you closed, we wouldn't have much of a town."

I wasn't overstating the case. The fact was, Little Bend was teetering between decline and renewal, though its condition was better than that of many of the state's small towns because of the tourist trade. Eric and Jane had been tourists themselves, bicycling across the state on the Katy Trail, when they stopped in the town for lunch and fell in love with the community.

I signed the debit slip. "Nobody likes his farm plan."

On Sunday, the next day, I put on my only suit and a tie and headed to town for Andre's funeral. An off-road truck splattered with mud forced me to slow down. A big black dog rode in the back, and a Confederate flag hung in the back window. A rifle rested in the gun rack.

I recognized Dwayne Hunthausen huddled over the wheel. He continued into town and along Main Street, then parked down from the General Store. The leader of a religious clan, he typically drove in only every few months. He mostly hid away with his followers in their compound, which lay in a valley at the end of a road to nowhere.

I pulled over to see what he was up to.

He got out of his truck. He was wearing military-style clothing and an Army cap. Like a soldier on patrol, he surveyed the street, his eyes darting from one building to another. He wasn't many years older than me, but his long and ragged beard made him appear older. Seeing him, an elderly woman leaving the café on Main Street hurried to her car, and a mother stepped out her front door and pulled her toddler back into their home.

He looked in my direction and I bent my head down.

When I looked up again, he was facing the other way. He returned to his truck and took the street leading to First Christian Church.

I followed.

When he approached the church, he slowed to a snail's pace and peered at the mourners entering the building.

He shouted something I couldn't make out.

Sarah was standing with several others in front of the white frame church, traditional with its steeple and arched windows and doors. A wooden sign proclaimed the church's name, the minister and the time of the Sunday service. Letters across the bottom announced: "All Are Welcome."

"What do you think he was doing here?" Sarah asked when I walked up to her.

"I don't know. I hope he's leaving town."

"He called us sodomites and harlots." She was amused. "Who is he?"

"Oh, a self-proclaimed minister and white supremacist. He and his survivalist followers—they call themselves the Sword of the Lord—live in the woods."

"He looks crazy."

"He is, believe me. Bat shit crazy."

"Nice suit. I hardly recognized you out of your camo outfit."

It was my turn to display chagrin.

The church had only a couple of dozen pews. Andre's mother and mourners from out of town sat in front, near a profusion of flowers banking the closed casket. Lyceum director Kelly Morgan also was near the front.

Harry and his wife Cheryl arrived and sat near the rear. Max entered and took a seat at the end of a pew.

When the Rev. Margot Laribee came in, her full figure was robed in black with a white stole. She led in singing the opening hymn, *Let Us Gather by the River.* Following the liturgy, she stepped up into the pulpit.

> *Friends, we are here to celebrate the life of a unique and talented individual who brought joy into the lives of many. I feel like I know Andre better in death than in life after*

hearing his many friends talk about his sense of fun and his love of life...

She made her eulogy brief, then welcomed mourners to share their stories about the deceased.

Kyle Hyde stood and paid tribute to Andre's dancing talent.

... His agility seemed effortless. None of us could match it. But I'll never forget his practical jokes. Once he put dog poop in the shoes of a director we all disliked...

Beginning to choke up, Hyde halted, then sat down.
When no one else rose to speak, Sarah did. She said Andre was like an uncle to her kids and mentioned that he had taken them to Royals baseball games.

He and Emily had a routine. If she had a red dress on, he'd say, "I like your blue dress." Emily would correct him, "It's not blue, it's red!"

They played this game again and again. My daughter loved it. And loved him.

A couple of other friends spoke, followed by David Schoenburg, the regional director of Planned Parenthood in Columbia.

Andre was a volunteer for our agency, and I always knew I could turn to him for a donation to assist a woman in trouble. He was too soft-hearted to say no. I liked him very much.

Recently he came to me and asked me what I thought about his chances to win a seat on the county commission. I told him I thought he should try and that taking a stand was as important as winning. I told him he could count on me for support.

I have been thinking about my advice over and over. As we all know there are those who hate men like Andre because of whom they love. If I had told him that it might be dangerous for him to seek public office would he still have run? I think we all know the answer to that.

Andre didn't let fear dictate his behavior.

I admit that, as someone who has received my share of hate mail and threats, I have had a few sleepless nights since his murder. But we need now to be resolute. We need to stand against hate. If we refuse to back off now, Andre's death will have meaning and leave us a powerful legacy.

When David took his seat, thoughtful silence filled the room.

Margot ended the service by reading a Langston Hughes poem and leading the assemblage in singing *Love Will Guide Us*.

Andre's mother, supported by two of his friends, led the procession out of the sanctuary.

Outside the church, Max approached Minnie Hadley. He and Andre's mother talked while walking to the parking lot.

11

The first thing next morning I phoned Margot to ask her to put me in touch with Minnie. But the minister said Minnie had already left for her home in New Orleans and she didn't have a number for her.

Then, about 9:30, while I was cleaning up from breakfast, Sarah called.

"Charles has been charged. Murder. First degree. I need to talk to you. Can you come to my office right away?"

I got dressed and didn't wear camouflage. Finding her law firm, 17 miles away in downtown Columbia, not far from the University of Missouri campus, was easy. Her office was on the first floor of a bunker-like, red-brick building with dark-tinted windows. The receptionist was an oh-so-proper woman who gathered her gray hair in a chignon. She greeted me with a smile and directed me to Sarah's corner office.

Sarah admitted me. She'd furnished the room in sleek contemporary Italian furniture, a world away from Little

Bend's obsession with all-things vintage.

"The results of the autopsy convinced Bill to bring the charges," she said. "Unlike what everybody assumed, Andre neither drowned nor was he strangled. There was no water in his lungs, so he was dead when he hit the river. Death was caused by a blow to the back of the head by a large object, probably a rock. That has made the prosecutor think that Andre was a victim of a confrontation that got out of control. He thinks Charles became enraged, lost control and struck Andre, killing him."

"What about the mutilation? Did the killer do that?"

"That was done with a knife, not by an animal. Andre was repeatedly slashed in the groin area."

"Don't that and the rope point to a hate crime?"

"You would think so, but Bill has a theory to explain that. He thinks Charles mutilated the body and tied the rope around Andre's neck after he had killed him to make the death appear to be a hate crime, to draw suspicion away from himself."

"Seems a stretch."

"In my years in court I've heard stranger things. Really."

"Well, how did Bill explain how the two happened to be out on the trail?"

"He suspects Charles was angry after their argument and followed him there when he saw Andre return for his bike."

"Have they found a murder weapon?"

"No. They think he probably threw it in the river, but if it was a rock...there're lots of rocks in the river. They've had divers out again but haven't found anything."

"What about Ralph's statement about a dog at the scene? Charles doesn't have a dog."

"The autopsy noted bites on the right calf made by a large animal, but the coroner couldn't determine what kind of animal or whether the bites were made before or after death. And the detective discounts Ralph's statement."

"So what do we do now?"

"You need to talk to Kelly. But then we must redouble our efforts to find the killer. Let's go through suspects one by one. Start with Max. The payments make him suspicious, and, remember, Andre was killed on the trail below his home."

"I tried to get in touch with Andre's mother this morning, but she's already on her way home. And I couldn't get a number for her."

"Good effort anyway. Until we can reach her, why don't you look around Max's property. Look for the bike. We know it's not in the river. If Max killed Andre, he may have hidden it in the yard."

"I'm not real comfortable with that. Max is my boss." It seemed disloyal to investigate him. I didn't mention that I was likely to lose my job if I was caught snooping.

But my reluctance made no impression on her whatsoever.

"I need to have you do this."

I acquiesced. "Yes, ma'am." The bar job was only temporary.

My sarcastic response irritated her. She pinned me, like a

bug on a board, with a piercing look.

"Watch for some time when the Arnauds are away."

I glanced out her window where some clients were walking by in the hallway. Sarah was now sitting with her legs crossed, a shoe dangling from her raised foot. I can't tell you how sexy that was.

"I've still got my eye on Russ too," she said. "In fact, he may be our top target."

"I'll Google him, and Max too. I might pull up something of interest."

"Yes, do that."

We spent some time talking about other suspects, including the man in the black truck and even Charles himself. But neither of us could imagine Charles as the murderer.

"What makes this investigation tough," she said, "is that anyone with an obsession with gays or blacks could have done it. It could be a pointless hate crime. In that case the killer is probably mentally ill. And there are enough eccentrics in this rural area that a deranged person wouldn't necessarily stand out.

"But let's proceed on the assumption that the killer is someone we can track down."

Upon leaving Sarah's office, I drove to Arrow Rock, the nearby restored historic village. Kelly was in her office at the theater. A perky woman in her 40s, she made me feel welcome at once. Though I was not acquainted with her, I knew she'd come from Rhode Island to take the theater position two years earlier.

"Thank you two for doing this!" she said when I said I was Sarah's investigator. "Charles really needs your help. We know he would never kill Andre."

She repeated what she'd told the deputies.

"Did Andre explain what the fight was about?"

"No, and I didn't want to pry into their relationship. We talked all night, but mostly about Andre's past and what he'd experienced, and his thoughts about life and what it all meant. He was having some sort of existential crisis, as if his life might be at a turning point. He was a very thoughtful person. And he was really bummed out. I told him he would see things differently in the morning, but he wasn't buying that. I tried to persuade him to go home and make up with Charles, but he absolutely wouldn't. He was in the same mood when he left in the morning."

"Did you think he might leave Charles, or even move out of the area?"

"Yes, maybe. But you know how lovers are when they're upset. A day or two can change everything."

"Did anything he said or do give you the idea that the fight might turn violent?"

"Oh, no. Nothing like that. He was just very sad."

As she said that, Kelly looked sad too. She was easy to like.

Once home, I typed "Russell Collins, Missouri developer" into Google and drew several men with that name. The second entry had the right address. The site gave only bare-bones information, but it told me Russ was a lawyer. He wasn't listed on the state bar roster, however.

I scanned further down the list of sites and found one other of interest: a *St. Louis Post-Dispatch* news article reporting Russ' conviction in 1991 for fraud in a Section 8 housing development in that city. He was sentenced to five years in prison.

That explained why he couldn't be a member of the bar.

Googling Max produced a newspaper story reporting that he had been accused by a client of misusing her money while he was a financial adviser in New Orleans. She'd filed a complaint with a state oversight board. Max, however, had repaid the client and the complaint was dropped.

The fact that Andre's mother also lived in New Orleans wasn't lost on me.

A profile of Max revealed he was a descendant of one of the early French pioneer families who settled along the Missouri. The Arnauds were trading with the Indians before Lewis and Clark made their journey up the river in 1804. When Max moved to Little Bend and opened the area's first Cajun restaurant he'd returned to his roots.

I emailed all the stories to Sarah.

When I reached Ralph Moon's trailer home, it appeared abandoned. A couple of its windows were boarded up, and a rag hung over another. The exterior was dirty and dented here and there. Weeds were growing headlong everywhere, except in some dirt patches in front of the door. Ralph's old bicycle was propped up next to the steps.

Knocking loudly on the door brought no answer. I was about to leave when Ralph stuck his head out the door. He was wearing long underwear that buttoned up the front, and he didn't say anything.

"I'd like to talk to you."

"What about?"

"About what you saw the morning Andre Hadley was killed."

He squinted in the sunlight, with a look of cunning.

"I already talked to the police."

"I know. They said you saw a man and a dog attack Andre. Can you describe the man?"

"Just a man. Strung the guy up. He was laughing at him and doing a jig."

"A jig?"

"Yeah. A jig. He was having fun."

"What else did you see?"

"Nothin. I got out of there. I didn't want trouble."

"Well, thanks for your time."

He continued to stare at me as I turned to leave. Ralph might be a hermit but he wasn't crazy. And it was possible he could identify the killer, if we could find him.

I headed off to work, feeling I'd earned my detective's salary.

On Tuesday, Mike Fowler, a contractor, came over to my place and gave me a hand as I worked on building a shop for my canoe business.

"He did it."

Mike was talking about Charles. He steadied the frame of a wall so I could nail it in place. Fresh sawdust floated in the air, infusing it with a sharp, clean smell.

"I'm sure he didn't." I sneezed.

"I don't get those boys," Mike said.

"There's nothing to get. The police got off track by arresting Charles. The real killer is going to get away. Or kill again."

"Maybe, but I still think Charles did it."

We let the conversation lapse. We weren't much alike but we'd been pals since high school and didn't need to talk. He'd been a good friend when everything was going wrong in my life and I needed a friend.

"We should go fishing. Hey, we should go noodling," Mike said after a while.

"I'm not doing that."

"You're a wuss," Mike joked.

Guys liked the sport because, in their mind, it was man against nature. Its danger only enhanced its appeal. To find catfish, they held their breath and swam underwater to hollow logs and holes in the bank where the fish lurked. The best spots were in Missouri River tributaries when the catfish were spawning. They stuck a hand in those places and waited for a big catfish to try to swallow it. Then they wrestled the fish to the surface.

I opposed noodling because it depleted the catfish breeding stock. And because it was illegal.

"We can't all be a real man like you."

Mike laughed derisively. Sometimes I didn't know why I put up with him.

We worked steadily throughout the morning, and by noon we were nailing the roof in place. When we finished, we stopped for a beer. Mike began to give me a hard time, as he regularly did, as we lounged on the porch.

"I hope you're getting in shape. The race is only two months away."

He was referring to the canoe marathon. We'd come in fifth the previous summer, our best result so far, and were planning to compete again that year.

I laughed and rolled up the sleeves on my smudged twill shirt. "You don't need to worry about me."

"I worry," Mike took a swig from his beer can. "You don't get much exercise standing behind that bar."

My phone rang. I took my boots off the railing and sat up in my chair.

Sarah's cultivated voice came through the cell phone.

"Jack, Sarah here. The Arnauds have gone into Beulah's BBQ. Why don't you check out their home now?"

"I'm gone."

"By the way, I asked Max why he had given money to Minnie Hadley. He wouldn't tell me, or confirm that he had done it."

12

The Arnauds lived in a low-slung 1950s house with an imposing front gate. I maneuvered my truck up a nearby lane and parked out of view in a soybean field. When I stepped onto the Arnauds' property, a black Lab began barking and raced toward me. I stood stock still and let him sniff me. He began wagging his tail.

The back lawn, covering several acres, ran unobstructed to the edge of the bluff, which rose straight up above the Katy Trail and the river. It was a dismal day, and an eerie mist still hovered over parts of the water, but below the oyster-colored sky I could still see the Missouri's brawny breadth curving like a giant snake far into the distance. I watched for a moment while an eagle glided along the river's edge.

The land on which I was standing was more than a hundred feet up, but a killer could have hidden down the hill, where the bluff shrank to a mound, and jumped down to attack a bicyclist. I scoured that corner of the yard, weaving through red buckeye shrubs, but found nothing.

I estimated I had 10 minutes before the Arnauds might return.

Thinking a bike could have been taken to the garage, I walked to its side door and entered it. A car approached on the road, and I stopped to listen and waited until it moved off into the distance.

There was no bike in the garage.

The door leading to the kitchen was unlocked. The ranch house had wide hallways and an open layout. The floors were tile and the furnishings modern. Glass cabinets displaying cocktail and wine glasses lined the wall leading to the dining room. In the living room a Collins glass with the remains of a drink and a paperback noir crime novel littered the sofa table; on the book's cover a woman was pulling up a dark stocking on her shapely leg. Broad windows looked out over the rear lawn.

A modern teak bed, low and wide, dominated the master bedroom, which had sliding glass doors opening onto a swimming pool. The bed was unmade. A bottle of Absolut sat on a chest of drawers. The scent of perfume teased my nose.

A matching desk sat against a wall. I pulled out its drawers one by one.

In the top left drawer was a bank book. Inside were a list of months by year and, to the right of them, sums transferred from one account to another. Always the same accounts. Most were about $500, but some were higher, one more than $7,600. They went back for 11 years. A quick mental tally put the total at more than $85,000.

I photographed the pages with my phone. I decided to go down to the basement. I figured I still had two minutes.

Lots of excellent wine. But no bike.

Another car now was approaching. After climbing the stairs, I slipped back into the garage. The car slowed and then the tires crunched the gravel on the driveway. I exited out the door I had come in and leaned back against the garage wall. When the car began to enter the garage, I scurried to my truck.

Then I phoned Sarah and told her about the bank book.

"It's a stretch, but those payments could be the money Max said he'd made to Minnie Hadley."

"Yes, that had occurred to me. You didn't find a bicycle?"

"No." I could sense her disappointment.

I was behind the bar that evening when Sarah walked in with a silver-haired older man, one almost as tall as me. Sarah introduced us.

"Jack, this is my dad. Jack is doing investigative work for me on the murder case."

I put out my hand. He shook it but, like his daughter when I'd first met her, looked like he'd rather not.

He exuded confidence. He managed to let me know I was a mere employee. But then he said in a booming voice: "I wish you could persuade Sarah to drop this murder defense.

It could be dangerous. But"—and here he smiled at Sarah —"she won't listen to me. I told her to not oppose the hog farm too. You can see how much good that did. It's not easy being a parent."

"Oh, Dad, you worry too much," Sarah said quietly. They had an understanding, one that kept me at a distance.

Then, turning to me, she said: "Dad's in town to buy a tapestry from Artful Antiques. He found it on the Internet. I arranged with Charles so we could get into the store and Dad could see it."

"Are you a collector?" I asked, just to be sociable.

"No." That put an abrupt end to conversation.

"It's beautiful and will be wonderful in the Kansas City house," Sarah said, smoothing over the awkwardness. "We're going to have dinner. Dad wants to try the roast pheasant. I need to talk with you. Come by the office tomorrow. Eleven o'clock."

I nodded.

Sarah had herself in tight control and appeared tenser than I'd ever seen her when I arrived in her office the next morning.

"You look stressed."

"It's the kids. Emily spilled milk on herself, and George locked himself in his room. You should try being a mom."

"Wrong gender." That made her laugh.

She offered to get me a soft drink. I declined.

"Well, I want one."

As she walked down the hall to the office refrigerator, I tagged along. "I hope you didn't let Dad's brusque manner put you off. He's a good guy—he just doesn't like to look like one."

She got out a bottled water. She then stopped at the receptionist's desk to ask Connie how her mother, who was apparently ill and in a nursing home, was doing.

Back in her office, Sarah said Charles' arraignment had taken place earlier that morning.

"Bond was set at $500,000. He can't raise the $50,000 to get out of jail. With his store struggling, he's overextended. I'd help him but legal ethics forbid that.

"But let's press ahead. We're not giving up on Russ or Max as suspects, but we should expand our investigation to include everyone we have questions about. I want you to check into Hunthausen and the Sword of the Lord. He or someone in his cult could be the killer. With their supremacist and bigoted views they might have targeted him."

For the first time, I perceived the flashing red light of danger ahead.

"I think nosing around the Sword of the Lord would be crazy. Dwayne Hunthausen is paranoid. And his group has lots of guns, probably dynamite too. For that matter, I don't know how I could get in. I've heard the compound is well guarded. The police should investigate them."

"Yes, but they won't. I talked to Shank about that

yesterday. He gave me the run-around. He apparently sees the group the way you do." Then she smiled cynically. "He also probably remembers the Branch Davidian fiasco. He doesn't want to set off something like that."

Shows he has good sense, I thought.

"I didn't want to put you in jeopardy," she said. "I queried some detective agencies about an investigation. But they turned me down. So now I have no choice. I'm down to you. We need to find out if anyone there was involved. Put your mind to it. You're clever. You can figure out a way to sneak in."

I looked at her in disbelief. Who did she think I was? Spiderman? But she was unfazed.

"I'll try to come up with a plan," I said, playing for time.

"There's one other thing," she said. "I got a threatening call yesterday. A crude-sounding man said, 'You don't want to be defending that homo,' and then hung up. Apparently somebody's trying to scare me off the case."

She laughed.

"I'm almost flattered. I didn't know anyone thought I was a threat as a defense lawyer!"

I smiled.

But then she stopped smiling: "He might try to get to you too, you know."

"Hmm." I remembered what was done to Andre. Then I thought about what that guy might do to Sarah—or me.

I decided to not think about that.

"Are you taking this threat seriously? You should, you

know."

"Yes. But I'm not dropping the case."

I knew she would say that.

13

I had plenty to think about as I drove home. I was becoming less interested in succeeding as a detective and more interested in not getting killed, or injured.

I hadn't thought much about the danger.

My phone rang as I was approaching Little Bend. It was Cheryl Bishop.

"Jack, I'm worried about my niece, Bonnie. She and her husband have gone to live with that religious community. You know all the terrible things we hear about that place. It's awful."

I did know the rumors. That Hunthausen coerced women in the group to sleep with him. That he beat the children, calling it discipline.

"Oh, I can understand your concern."

"I'm her closest relative, but she didn't listen to me when I tried to talk her out of her nutty idea. Now she wants to leave, even if she has to separate from her husband. But she's afraid to."

"Have you talked to the police?"

"They won't do anything. They think this is a domestic matter. They say Bonnie has to ask them for help, and she won't do that, or I have to have evidence that something is wrong. Do you think you could find a way to get her out?"

Forces seemed to be conspiring to get me into the compound. I hadn't said no to Sarah, though I was still thinking about it. But it was harder to turn down Cheryl. Her appeal came from the heart and I owed her. When my mother ran off, Cheryl and Harry took me in. Gave me odd jobs, so I could supplement the money Mom left me. She and Harry were the closest thing I had to family.

"I suppose I could go out there, though I'm not sure what good it will do."

"Oh, would you? I'd feel so much better knowing we're doing what we can."

"What's Bonnie's number? Maybe she can suggest a way I can get in."

"You can't get her on the phone. I can't call her either. When I call the compound, they say there's no Bonnie there. I imagine she's taken a new name. I have to wait for her to call. I only know she wants out because she phoned me last night."

After getting off the phone with Cheryl, I needed to clear my head and think about how to approach Sword of the Lord.

I drove into town and turned onto the first side street, gliding down the gentle hillside past the town's showcase yellow Victorian home to the city park, where I pulled onto the grass. The day had turned warm, and I rolled down my side window for air.

I slouched back in the seat and, rather than mull over the cult, my thoughts drifted to Sarah. I recalled her direct gaze and her crooked, mocking smile and the way she stood as she looked into the distance at the cancer party. And how she looked with her hair up....

Then I pulled myself back. What was I doing? She was too old for me. As if she would be interested in me anyway.

I thought about how dismissive of me she was. But a moment later I was staring up into the blue sky and conjuring up Sarah's face and the benign lightness of her gray-green eyes. Those magical eyes that radiated amused pleasure.

You're a fool, I told myself. But, the thing was, I didn't mind being one.

Near me in the park boys were playing baseball. One of them was George, Sarah's son. A fly ball drifted out to him in right field and he dropped it. Embarrassed, he looked down and kicked the dirt. I had to smile, recalling my own boyhood experiences on the ball diamond. Though I played team sports, I was mediocre, except at basketball, where my height gave me an edge.

When George came up to bat, he took a strike, swung at the next pitch and missed, then hit the third pitch just over the shortstop's head. He raced off to first base, started toward second and fell. The first baseman tagged him out.

His teammates began to take the field, but when George didn't get up they clustered around him. He was holding his ankle.

"What's wrong, Georgie?" I heard the team's pitcher, an older and taller kid with spiky hair, ask. "You hurt yourself? Don't be a faggot. Run it out."

The pitcher gave George a push.

George took a limping step then stopped in pain. A couple of his teammates laughed. The pitcher pushed him again, George pushed back and the pitcher hit him in the stomach. George bent over, struggling for breath, then stood up and raised his fists, his lips quivering.

I stepped out of the truck.

"George, I told your mother I'd take you home."

George looked over at me, confused, then hobbled over. He got into the truck without saying anything. He wiped his eyes with his small fists and looked up at me.

"That was a pretty good hit you got."

George nodded.

"You weren't supposed to get me. Mom said I should go to Cheryl's."

"That's true, but I thought it was time for you to get out of there. You've got some nasty pals."

I took out my phone and pressed the app for monitoring police calls. There was buzzing, then "DUI at I-70 and 240."

"What's that?"

"A police scanner app." George looked impressed.

I smiled to myself, shut off the monitor and phoned Sarah, catching her at home. I explained the situation.

"I'll drop him off. A doctor should probably look at his ankle."

The sky had become overcast and threatening by the time we turned into the farm. I helped George limp toward the front door. Sarah opened it before we reached it and kneeled down to embrace George, but he stood up straight and brushed her off, saying, "I'm okay, Mom."

She looked at George with concern.

"Are you really okay?" she asked, bending over him.

"I'm all right, MOM!" he said loudly while pulling away from her.

Sarah then looked at me, her face showing gratitude. She asked me in and offered me ice tea. Her home was straight out of a magazine. Only the school books and papers scattered about showed that real people lived there.

"What happened?" she asked.

I told her how George fell rounding first base.

She offered me more ice tea.

I declined. "I've got to get back to the bar."

14

The entrance had no marking.

As I turned onto the rutted drive, I remembered that the Sword of the Lord believed a race war was coming that would usher in the end time. They were stocking up on supplies to wait out the war, which would go global.

Pessimistic folks.

The meandering trail continued for more than a half mile into a valley overgrown with vegetation. The place was the definition of remote.

I should have brought a gun, I thought. I also had second thoughts about taking the direct approach and driving in unannounced.

Around a curve, a jumble of windowless metal buildings appeared close ahead in a clearing in the forest. Children were playing in an open area in the center of the complex, from which rose a tall, rough-hewn wooden cross. Several women wearing scarves and long dresses walked from one building to another, and a couple of bearded men were on a roof, working on it. Seeing me, the men disappeared down the back of the building and the women gathered up the children and hustled inside the largest building, which stood behind the cross.

A sign posted on the building's front laid out 15 rules or biblical quotes. The first: *No talking after sunset.* Another: *Behold, I will make them of the synagogue of Satan, which say they are Jews, and are not, but do lie. Revelations, 3:9.*

I walked up to the front door and opened it. Inside were rows of wooden benches where a couple of dozen people sat, the women on the left and men on the right. The women had their heads covered with scarves or bonnets, and the men were bearded and dressed in farm clothes. Several had turned around and were looking at me. One child sucked her thumb while watching me.

The room was silent.

Against the wall in the front of the building, apparently a chapel, was a large painting of Jesus with seven stars in his right hand and a two-edged flaming sword coming out of his mouth. Across the top in gilt letters was written: Repent; or else I will come unto thee quickly, and will fight against them with the sword of my mouth.

Hunthausen stood before the painting, next to a lectern.

"Come in, brother," he said. "Do you want to join us?"

"No. I want to talk to Bonnie."

"No one here has that name, and we don't let strangers wander around. There are some who would hurt us."

"I'm harmless." I raised my arms and showed my open palms. "I have a message for Bonnie from her aunt."

"If you don't want to become one of us, you have to leave."

He was firm about that, plainly ready to enforce his statement. It seemed wise to not test his resolve.

"Okay, I'm sorry to have disturbed you."

Outside, the clearing remained empty. There seemed nothing to do but drive out. But when I was back on the county road, I pulled off to the side and parked. Cheryl and Sarah wouldn't want to hear I'd quietly obeyed Hunthausen's order and left. I got out and skirted through the woods, following the line of the driveway back toward the chapel. This area had been logged before, and brush now thrived. Brambles tugged at my clothing in the undergrowth, and I had to climb repeatedly over fallen trees. Flies and mosquitoes, too thick to brush away, buzzed around my face.

When I reached a ridge, I took it, finding the going easier. Soon buildings appeared through the foliage.

I crept closer, not far from a path running between two buildings. Two men came out of one of the buildings and walked toward the other. I hunkered down out of sight. Soon three women approached from the other direction. I swatted at the flies hovering around my face.

A boy, maybe six or seven, wandered in my direction. He was carrying a stick and swinging it at the taller grasses in some sort of game of his own imagination. I stood up with my hands in my pockets, trying to look friendly.

"Hey, can I play too?"

He looked warily at me.

"Look, I have something for you." I took out my Swiss pocket knife and showed it to him, pulling the blades and tools out one by one. His eyes got big.

"You know who Bonnie, the new woman, is?"

He nodded.

"If you'll go find her and bring her to me, and not tell anybody else I'm here, I'll give you this knife."

He ran off.

I swatted some more flies and tried to ignore the strain in my legs from crouching. The minutes ticked by interminably.

Then the boy reappeared, holding the hand of a woman wearing a red scarf and a long calico dress. She was an older and heavier version of the Bonnie who had been my class-mate.

"Do you know who I am?" I asked.

She nodded. "Did Cheryl send you?"

"Yes. She says you want to leave."

"It's terrible here. I have to work all the time. I'm just a drudge. And when I complain they hit me. And that's not the worst. I don't even get to see John." That was her husband. "He sleeps in the men's house."

When another woman exited one of the buildings, Bonnie looked around nervously.

"You have to go," she said.

Before she could say anything more the woman called

out: "Who are you talking to?"

"An old high school friend."

"That's against the rules. He can't be here." She turned and shouted: "Jesse! John! There's a man here!"

Then she began to run back to the building she'd come from. Before she reached it, a pickup pulled up near me and two men got out. One took an assault rifle from the rack in the truck.

Another truck was also driving in my direction.

"Get down on the ground," the man with the gun said.

It seemed smartest to comply. Four men now circled around me. One of them put a knee into my back and another put his foot on my neck. They twisted my arms behind my back and tied them and my legs together with rope.

That didn't feel good.

One kicked me several times in the ribs with his heavy boots. That felt worse.

"That's for sneaking around. If you do it again, there'll be more."

They waited, not saying anything more. Within a few minutes, Hunthausen showed up. The guards pulled me up to face him. He had been a sickly misfit as a boy, but now he was rugged.

"What are you doing back here?" he snapped. Beads of sweat had broken out on his forehead.

"Do you know who I am?" I asked, trying to engage him in conversation. "I was in Gary's class." Gary was his brother.

He nodded faintly. "You have no business talking to

Bonnie."

"Her aunt is worried about her. She wanted me to check on her."

"Tell her she's fine."

"Some say you killed Andre Hadley."

His face went blank like a TV set losing power.

"They're lying. I didn't have nuthin' to do with that." He pulled back and his eyes narrowed, like a trapped animal's. Then he reached over and seized me by the throat.

"You're lucky we don't shoot you. We know what to do with evil people like you."

Hearing that once was enough to convince me.

He turned to the men. "Throw him out."

Bonnie was watching from the path, her expression giving away nothing.

"Call me," I mouthed, as the men grabbed me and threw me into the back of one of the trucks. That made the pain peak again.

It got worse as we bounced down the bumpy lane and out onto the county highway. After a few minutes, the driver slowed and the two men watching over me in the truck bed tossed me out onto the roadside.

I felt every stick and rock as I rolled over the shoulder and down an embankment. When the pain and shock ebbed enough that I could move, I worked at the knot on my wrists until I freed my hands. I was bleeding from scratches on my arms and face. I untied my legs and crawled out of the ditch and made my way to my truck.

Tough-guy Philip Marlowe would have shrugged all this off. But I wasn't Philip Marlowe. My entire body ached.

I felt like a flop as a friend and an investigator. I hadn't rescued Bonnie and I knew nothing more about whether the Sword of the Lord had killed Andre.

All I'd discovered was that the men of the clan were brutal enough to commit murder.

Back at home, I fell into bed. When I woke up, it was nearly five o'clock. I called the restaurant, said I was sick and wouldn't be coming in that night. I washed the dirt and blood off myself and then phoned Sarah to report in.

I left out my treatment by the men. I didn't want her pity.

"You should have tried to talk to other people there," she said.

I explained why that wasn't possible. Her silence made me think she didn't have a high opinion of my explanation.

That irked me, motivating me to point out: "By the way, Max couldn't have killed Andre."

"Why not?"

"He was with Angelica that night and until noon the next day."

"How do you know?"

"Angelica told me. Last night as we were closing up."

15

When I got into my truck the next forenoon, a baseball glove was sticking out from under the passenger's side of the seat. Its small size made me smile.

"Sarah," I said when I got her on the phone, "George left his glove in my truck. Should I bring it by?"

"I am at the office, and there's no reason for you to drive this far. Will you be at the bar this afternoon?"

"I'm off today."

"I could pick it up at your house on my way home."

"Sure," I said. I gave her directions to my place.

"I'll be there about four."

She was as good as her word. When I looked out the window as the clock struck four, I saw her Volvo turn into my driveway, which was only a sandy lane with weeds in the middle. It occurred to me that she might not think much of my home. The house was small and needed paint, and was way down the economic ladder from hers. I thought about the two weather-beaten chairs and the metal TV tray on the front porch.

When I opened the aluminum storm door to let her in, I noticed again the rip in the screen.

Well, I wasn't going to apologize for my home.

She didn't inquire about the scrape on the side of my face, though she must have seen it. I concluded she didn't realize how I got it and didn't want to embarrass me by asking. I supposed she thought I had gotten into a scrap at the bar, or had done something equally disgraceful.

She was reserved and businesslike as she took in the living room with the sling chair, my old couch, the scratched-up upright piano and the boxes of books stacked along the walls. (I'd intended to unpack them but never gotten around to it.)

But she focused on my grandfather clock.

"That's a beautiful piece."

"I inherited it from my mother. It came down through her family."

She took in the tinted Victorian photo of my great-grandmother and the letter of another ancestor's acceptance into the Union Army.

"You appreciate your family's heritage."

"Yeah, that's true." I smiled and offered her a drink.

"Four's a little early, but why not?"

I invited her to come into the kitchen while I made it.

"Martini?" That's what she'd been drinking the night of the gala.

"Yes."

I recalled that she wanted two olives. So I put two in her drink.

"You remembered." She'd taken a stool at my island.

I made a Manhattan for myself, then took the other stool.

"You have lots of books."

"Quite a few. Some were my mother's."

"Does she live around here?"

"She died three years ago."

"Oh, I'm sorry."

"She had cancer."

"That must have been hard on you."

"It was." I wasn't about to tell her about how my mother had abandoned me, then returned when she got her diagnosis. "I dropped out of college to be with her. It's not easy to watch a person dying by inches."

"Did you go back to school?"

"I got my degree in ecology two years ago."

"What about your father? Is he alive?"

"He died of a heart attack, when he was only 52."

"So you're alone."

She changed the subject.

"I appreciate so much what you did for George. I saw the bruise on his chest last night, and he told me about the fight. He cried in remembering it. You should have told me. I am his mother. But I suppose you men have to keep your secrets."

She was almost coy as she said that. I let her interpret my reticence however she wished.

"I'd like to show my gratitude in a more tangible way.

We've planned a family picnic along the river this weekend. Would you join us?"

"That'd be nice."

She crossed her legs, catching my eye. She noticed and smiled. I smiled too.

"We have a development in the murder case," she said.

"I thought the murder might come up."

"Max has put up the money for Charles' bond."

I was taken back. "What? Why did he do that?"

"He wouldn't explain his reasons, and he would only give the money to me if I promised not to make his assistance public. So keep mum about it."

"Did you ask him for the money?"

"No. We were working out the details of the Planned Parenthood fundraiser when he asked me about Charles and the strength of our defense. Then he said he'd put up the bail. I can't make any sense of it. Can you?"

"No. It's baffling."

I mulled over this turn of events for a moment.

"We have to find out about those payments in the bank book," I said, thinking aloud, "but I'm clueless how we can do that."

"I may know a way."

I waited for her to say more. But she didn't. Ever the cryptic Sarah.

She changed the topic again.

"Have Angelica and Max been an item long?"

"A couple of months. I know Max's an older guy, but it's

a steamy affair from what Angelica says. The other day they had sex at dawn on Max's balcony."

Sarah smiled.

"He keeps her underpants," I added. "She has to be one of Victoria Secret's best customers."

Sarah erupted into laughter. Her boisterousness gobsmacked me. Who would have thought she could so completely abandon her buttoned-down demeanor?

"Thanks for the research on Max and Russ," she said. "It's more intriguing than ever now. Particularly Russ' past. The mystery gets ever murkier."

I waited, aware that she was thinking and would have more to say.

"I've decided that we have to look into the rumors of illegalities in county government. It's possible—perhaps even likely—that if they are true the corruption is connected to Andre's slaying. I think that all the more after learning about the developer's checkered past.

"You're local. Do you think we have crooked officials?"

"Well, everyone knows Hal's the political boss here. And he's a sleazy guy. I guess that explains some of his support. He's arranged parties with strippers for sheriff's deputies. One caused quite a scandal when a Columbia columnist got wind of it and wrote about it."

"That's disgusting, but it doesn't rise to the level of serious corruption."

"No, but who knows what other shady stuff he's involved in. He's heavy-handed. Most people think it's dangerous to cross him."

"Is there evidence of that?"

"Not that I know of. But some believe he's gotten people who opposed him fired from their jobs. And most everyone agrees that you have to get along with him to get anything done. The rumors are that he takes money under the table. Is it true? Got me."

"Might Russ have paid off Hal for the right vote on the hog farm?"

"I wouldn't be surprised. Remember their meeting. That vote shouldn't have gone the developer's way."

"Why do you say that?"

"I'd heard before the hearing that the plan would be rejected. And nothing during the hearing would have swayed the commission to support the project, in my opinion."

"Wouldn't Russ have had to pay off the other commissioners?"

"I doubt it. The word is that if Hal tells the other commissioners to vote for something, they fall in line. Except for Darlene, who votes the way she wants."

We got up and moved out of the kitchen.

"I think I'll talk to Bill," she said.

She looked around the living room again. Her face was a mask but I thought it disguised disapproval.

"I'll get the glove."

"Thanks," she said as I handed it to her. She couldn't have appeared more gracious.

16

The next day, Sunday, was routine through my shift at the bar. On my way home I started up the scanner app, but the chatter was only about a woman frightened by a drunken vagrant walking down the street.

Those were nerve-wracking days for Little Bend.

I had been avoiding talking to Cheryl about the dead-end I had encountered at the Sword of the Lord, but I couldn't put that off any longer so I stopped at her place. I also wanted to return Harry's Yamaha outboard, which I had repaired and had in my truck. I was toting it to their garage when Cheryl turned on the front porch lights of the old Victorian house.

She walked out and waved.

"Is it too late? I got the motor running."

"Come in and talk to me," she shouted.

Cheryl was a plain-spoken and serious woman in her 60s. She parted her steel-gray hair in the middle and chopped it at chin level. She couldn't have cared less about fashion.

I followed her into the kitchen.

"What happened to you?" She had gotten a look at my face.

"A little tussle."

"You guys!" she said, sparing me both any judgment or cloying concern.

After she heard about my trip to the compound and my brief encounter with Bonnie, she smiled. "You tried. That's all you could do."

That was Cheryl. Always putting people at ease.

Too tired to put my truck in my garage, I left it in the driveway when I got home. The decrepit building let in rain and daylight from where roof shingles were missing so it wasn't much protection anyway. Andre's murder was on my mind, and the image of his water-logged body resurfaced in my consciousness as I walked to the front door. It was ajar, which was odd.

I pushed the door open and listened. My eyes adjusted, taking in the moonlight coming through the side window of my living room. Stepping inside, I watched for movement. Not seeing anything, I flipped on the lights. All appeared normal.

I went to the kitchen and took a bottle of whiskey from the shelf and poured myself a drink. Then I moved on to my bedroom. My desk had been rummaged. Drawers hung out. My checkbook and some receipts lay on the carpet. In the bookcase a shelf was empty, the shelf where I kept my bird-count notebooks.

I checked my gun cabinet, but it hadn't been tampered

with.

Nothing appeared to be missing except the notebooks.

When I turned on the back porch light, Buddy came out from under the stoop and looked up.

"A fine watchdog you are." He wagged his tail.

Returning to the living room, I turned out the lights and moved to a window. I scanned the field leading to the road. All was still.

On Monday morning, I drove to Little Bend's police station. When I walked in, Cudinhead nodded. Apparently my involvement in the murder investigation was making him less hostile.

When he got a good look at my face, he gave me his full attention.

"What happened to you?"

"I fell."

"It must have been some fall."

Having no interest in confiding in him, I moved on to the purpose for my visit, telling him about the burglary.

"Well, you need to make out a report." He pulled out a form and pushed it in my direction.

"This break-in may be related to the murder," I said when I'd filled out all the blanks.

"Maybe so, maybe not. Perhaps you're imagining things, like everyone else. The town is scared. The sheriff had a line of people wanting concealed-carry permits after you found the body. He's never had more than one at a time before." He looked directly at me. "We need to close the book on this homicide, before we have jumpy people shooting each other."

He was getting downright chatty. And I noticed the plural pronoun. Evidently he thought he was in on the investigation.

I double-checked the report form to make sure it was complete. I pushed the form back to him. "There you are."

Cudinhead looked it over. "All that's missing are some notebooks?"

"That's right."

"What's in them?"

"My bird survey records."

"Well, if that's all you lost, you're lucky."

17

The week's *Murray County Trader* lay unread on my kitchen table the next morning as I sipped my coffee. The murder charge against Charles was its lead story, and an inset directed readers to the editor's column. I flipped to it.

> *The murder of performer Andre Hadley has sent shock waves through the community. Little Bend has enjoyed a reputation as a quiet and safe town with almost no crime. So a homicide here is out of character.*
>
> *The slaying appears to be the community's first since the founding of this newspaper in 1949. A review of the newspaper's files turned up no other murder cases.*
>
> *Commendably, the investigation by local law enforcement has led to the arrest of a suspect. There should be no rush to judgment. The legal system must be given time to work. But the quick action by authorities should reassure residents, who were understandably alarmed that a killer was at large in the community.*

Charles must be guilty if residents can now relax, I mumbled to myself with disgust. There was more to the editorial, but its content was conventional.

I took a gulp of coffee and tossed the paper back down on the table. My cat Dusty caught my eye when she began to paw something white on the floor underneath the overhang of a kitchen cabinet. I started to reach down, forgetting my ribs were still sore, but the stabbing pain made me instantly sit upright. Kneeling down, I picked up the object. Powder in a plastic bag.

Puzzled at first about where it came from, I then realized the intruder may have dropped it.

Or planted it.

Aware the bag could be evidence in the burglary, I put it in a paper sack and set it on the counter. I took the sack with me when I left for town then made the police station my first stop. Talk radio's Rush Limbaugh was on the air haranguing against liberals. Pansies, he called them.

"Do you know anything yet about the burglary?" I asked Cudinhead.

"I've got bigger fish to fry right now. It's not on the top of my list."

I handed him the sack. "I found that in my kitchen. It looks like meth to me. Maybe the intruder left it."

"You sure it isn't yours?"

I ignored him and his knowing smile.

"Well, I'll check it out and see what it is."

Hazy clouds drifted in the lambent sky later that morning while I peered through the binoculars looking for birds in the marsh. The theft of the notebooks hadn't hindered my research as I had been transferring the data to a spread sheet on my laptop. I was glad now for that precaution, and not just because of the money. Rumor had it that businessmen were considering putting a resort or some other commercial venture on the bank there. They liked the access—Interstate 70 was only a few minutes away. Environmentalists opposed development along the river, and my survey could be some of the evidence, if it was needed, of the value of these wetlands to local wildlife.

I had been bird watching for only a few minutes when I spotted an unexpected species—and not avian. On low-lying land at the edge of the marsh stood two men. Adjusting the binoculars to bring them into focus I recognized Russ.

The other guy was tall with gray hair. I couldn't see his face.

I watched them until they walked off.

I finished my day's survey and thoughtfully started home. Wind from the southwest roughed up the main channel, capping the waves with white water. As my boat plowed through the waves, spray came over the gunwale, showering me and Buddy, who sat in the front seat, his ears blown back by the wind.

I pondered Russ' presence near the marsh. He could be planning a development there. He appeared to have few scruples. Then I thought about the theft of my notebooks. It was logical to think that he wouldn't be above arranging a burglary. For that matter, of course, he might not be above murder.

I was becoming convinced I needed to get to the bottom of the burglary. Since the constable showed little interest, I decided to look into it myself.

After all, I was now a detective. Right?

18

When I went shopping on Wednesday forenoon, Margot was in the General Store along with another shopper, a mousy woman I recognized as Russ' wife. She left their farmhouse so seldom that people joked Russ must keep her locked up. I'd never seen her out, except to buy groceries.

She avoided eye contact as usual.

I'd just picked out a head of lettuce when Bonnie walked in, followed by two bearded men. When she saw me, she looked away and started down an aisle. The men, who were now eyeing me, stayed back by the front door.

Margot walked over to me.

"Isn't that Bonnie, Cheryl's niece?"

"Yes."

She looked thoughtful, and then, without saying a word, walked toward Bonnie and began examining canned goods. The two of them started whispering.

Margot, after putting tomatoes in her basket, marched

back to the front counter, where Cudinhead was chatting with Eric. She paid for her groceries, then turned to the constable.

"Chuck, my car engine is making a strange noise. Would you come out and listen to it for me? Maybe you can tell me if I have a problem?"

Eric smiled at Cudinhead, who said agreeably, "Sure."

Soon Margot and Cudinhead walked back into the store. "He's good, you know," she said to Eric. "He knew what the problem was right away...I forgot something."

But instead of doing more shopping, she went into the restroom at the back of the store. In a moment, Bonnie followed her there. There was the sound of breaking glass.

The men who had been watching became alarmed and started moving toward the restroom. But when they reached the end of the aisle, their way was blocked by the constable.

"Where you boys going? What's your hurry?"

The first of the men looked down at the constable's oversized girth, which filled the aisle. The man looked as if he was trying to decide whether he could get by Cudinhead if the constable turned sideways.

He then looked at the second man, who looked at Cudinhead, then his badge and shrugged. The first man swiveled and hurried back down the aisle, with the other man at his heels.

I heard a screech and saw Margot's car racing away from the store. Cudinhead was watching too, a smile on his face.

He strolled over to me. "I've seen everything now. She's one gutsy woman."

"Yes."

"She just rescued Bonnie. Her aunt was worried about her and wanted to get her away from that cult."

That afternoon I called Cheryl and asked her to put Bonnie on the phone. But that was another dead end. Bonnie said the men in the clan believed the police might try to storm their compound, so they were stockpiling weapons and ammunition and doing drills after morning prayers in preparation for an assault. But she hadn't heard anything about anyone in the group being involved in Andre's death.

Betty Young, my neighbor across the road, answered my knock quickly the next morning.

"Hi, neighbor," I said.

The 86-year-old widow had bright, birdlike eyes that reflected her mental acuity. I hadn't talked to her in a while, but I saw her some mornings when she walked to her mailbox in her pink terry cloth bathrobe to get her mail. "Come in. You want a cup of coffee?"

"Thanks, but I just had one. How are you?"

"I'm doing well. My daughter checks in on me every day. She makes sure I take care of myself."

"Someone broke into my home. The day after I found Andre's body. You didn't by any chance notice anything suspicious about that time, did you?"

"There was an old truck in your yard."

"What time was that?"

"I'm not sure. It was dark out. I had gone to bed early, and a noise woke me up. I went to see what it was. You'll find out when you're my age that you don't sleep too well. A man got out. It seemed late, but I thought he was visiting you."

"No, I must have been at work. Can you describe him?"

"He had long hair. You know, with a ponytail, like a hippy. I saw him when he went by your yard light."

I knew who that would be. I thanked her as I opened the door to leave. "Remember, if you need anything, you can always call me."

I phoned Sarah. As her employee, I had an obligation to tell her about the break-in. She'd also want to know about Russ at the marsh and Bonnie's rescue.

She scolded me about my delay in telling her about the burglary. "You should have told me earlier. Was anything stolen?"

"Yes, the notebooks where I kept my bird records."

"But your notebooks! You lost all your work!"

"Actually, I didn't." I explained about how I'd been transferring the data.

Then I mentioned who I suspected was behind the break-in. I told her as well about my interview with Bonnie.

"That's disappointing," she said.

But she perked up when I mentioned seeing Russ at the marsh.

"I'd like to know more about that. Do you know how you can find out who owns that land?"

"I imagine the Recorder's Office can tell me. I'll get on that tomorrow. There was another guy with Russ," I added. "He was tall with gray hair." I now remembered who the man resembled. "He looked a little like your father."

"It couldn't have been Dad. He has better things to do than tramp through this rural area. Besides, if he were here, he would have visited me."

Feeling discouraged, I decided to take a drive. I headed to the Katy Trail access area near where I had discovered Andre's body and turned in. A gentle rain had stopped, the sun had come out again, and the temperature was reaching into the 70s. A scent of cedar was in the air and a little wind was blowing as I got out of the truck and began hiking down the trail toward the murder scene. Locust trees, showing green buds, cast shadows that swung back and forth across the ground.

The bicycle tracks remained visible at the side of the gravel path. They ran into grass and brush and disappeared. I noticed a muddle of large dog tracks too; Ralph had it right. Bark had been worn off the lowest branch of a nearby oak.

The turgid river was up on the bank. A gust of wind came up, swaying the pawpaws with their burgundy flowers and bringing their foul odor.

19

Dusty circled my head, nudging me, on the morning of the picnic. She wanted her food. I turned over, and when I did, Buddy stuck his nose in my face.

I groaned. "Enough."

I got dressed with the cat winding through my legs. When I raised the shades, bright sunlight flooded the room. Dusty strolled to a light shaft and rolled in it on the floor. When it was time to leave, I grabbed a hat, sunglasses and a beach towel, picked up the only bottle of wine in my cupboard and carried them to my truck.

The scanner app revealed only vandalism to an auto.

Sarah's driveway was shaded by the Osage-orange trees lining each side and emerged onto a sunny lawn. Her station wagon was parked in the porte cochere. In the bright morning light, the mansion's white paint gleamed. The structure's architecture was classic—columns at the two-story entrance, tall windows with shutters flanking each side on each level and a widow's walk capping the roof.

Sarah came out and waved as I got out of my truck. She'd tied her shirt in front, exposing her midriff, and pulled her hair back, capturing it with a red scarf.

"You're in time to help pack up the car!" she announced.

When I got up to the porch, she said: "The kids won't be coming. I hope you don't mind. Clark called to say he can't return them until 9 o'clock this evening."

Clark was her ex. I absorbed that news with relief. Entertaining children wasn't my forte. And, to be honest, I wasn't unhappy with having a chance to be alone with Sarah.

"That's so like Clark!" she said. "So much for the family outing!"

"What have you planned?"

"Why don't we stroll down the Katy Trail and find a sandy place along the shore? Can you find a spot where we can walk down to the water? I love the river."

"Sure. That's perfect."

"We can take my car."

Her entryway was large, leading to a grand, curving stairway. Sarah walked over and touched me on the arm, which got my full attention.

"The cooler's in the kitchen." She pointed to the doorway at the side of the staircase. "You can also bring the picnic basket."

When we were on our way, I asked about Charles.

"I saw him downtown Wednesday," I said.

"He's been out since Monday, when the bond was posted.

He's doing better, though he's still stressed out. I've never seen a man so relieved to be out of jail. He wanted to know who put up the bail money and didn't want to accept my answer that I couldn't say.

"He said, in that emphatic way of his: 'You mean I have a friend I'm not aware of? Very mysterious, but thank God.'

"I have enjoyed Charles' company," she added, "more than that of anyone else in town. He's so witty and well read, and I have found his conversation stimulating. And he's also been a very good friend. When I moved here after my divorce he listened with endless patience as I ranted on about my ex-husband and his infidelities.…

"That reminds me of something he told me then: 'You can't trust men to be faithful.' "

She looked thoughtful.

I told her I'd returned to the scene of the murder.

"I saw dog tracks there. I don't think the police took casts of them. They're eroded now."

"The deputies aren't quite professional," Sarah said. "I sometimes wonder if the sheriff's department is corrupt too."

"I put it down to incompetence."

We rode quietly for a moment. "When I talked to Bill," she said, "he was interested to hear about Russ' past. I asked him about the rumors floating around the commission. He wouldn't confirm them—he has to be careful as prosecutor—but he also didn't deny that there might be something to them. He suggested I talk to Darlene Spencer, which was damn helpful of him. Didn't you say you knew her?"

"Yes, she and my mother were friends. She's a hoot—and no fool."

"I want you to interview her. See what you can find out."

"All right."

"I know, one more trail to chase down. We seem unable to rule out any suspects or make progress in our investigation. But we have to keep checking out all leads. Something will break."

I had to admire her. When she was on a mission, she was driven.

We had arrived at the trail parking lot. After we strolled a ways down the trail, the sight of a stretch of barren shoreline, coursing water and warm sun dispelled the threatening cloud of the murder. Sarah spread out a blanket by a driftwood log.

"I haven't had an outing like this since my divorce," she said.

The topic was outside my experience, but I made a stab at continuing the conversation.

"I guess getting divorced is tough."

"That's an understatement. Clark left me no choice but to divorce him. He had affairs, repeatedly. When I found out he said he was sorry and wouldn't betray me again. But he did. He didn't seem to think the affairs mattered. I was supposed to overlook them.

"But the worst was that he lied to me."

"I know guys like that." I didn't say some of them were friends. "You were smart to leave him."

"Thank you for saying that."

She looked pensive.

"The divorce was upsetting for the children." She said that more to herself than me.

She opened the picnic basket, then spread a blue-and-white checked tablecloth on the blanket and set out dishes and napkins. She put out peaches, vegetables and cherry-glazed game hens with rice stuffing.

I couldn't wait to dig in. "What a scrumptious picnic."

She smiled as we watched the river roll by.

"A red-tail." I pointed at a hawk that had soared in, pulling up in a dead tree.

"You like birds."

"I'm a birder."

"How many species have you identified?"

"Three hundred and thirteen."

"Wow. Impressive."

"I want to work in wildlife management or conservation —out of doors. But there have been no job openings recently, with both the state and federal government cutting back."

"You love this area? You planning to stay here?"

"I'd like to. My dream is to work around the Missouri."

"Why?"

"Oh, lots of reasons. The river's got fascinating birds and fish. Some are threatened."

"Like what?"

"Well, the pallid sturgeon. It's on the endangered species list."

"Why is it special?"

"It's a relic from the dinosaur age. It has cartilage plates under its skin that are sort of like armor, instead of bones or scales. It lives a long time, up to one hundred years, and can grow up to five feet long and weigh as much as 85 pounds.

"It's a bottom feeder and really ugly. It has a long flat snout like the shovelnose, if you're familiar with that. That's a smaller relative."

"Hmm, I guess you never know what might be lurking in the river."

"True enough."

We took our wine glasses, and I followed her upriver. Out in the water the head of an otter popped up. It made a clicking noise.

"She's warning us off." I laughed. "Her home must be nearby."

"She's darling. I love otters."

"Why did you become a lawyer?"

"I wanted to fight to see the right thing done." She appended a self-deprecating laugh. "I wanted to help the powerless. You know, the idealist thing. I know what people think of lawyers. But we're not all cynical."

We had reached the driftwood remains of a large fallen tree that lay out over the water. Sarah stepped onto its sun-bleached trunk and walked on it out over the water to better view the river. Her blouse flapped in the wind above her shorts, and she shielded her eyes with her hand.

"I don't think I could ever get tired of looking at the river," she said.

When she stepped back off the trunk, she surprised me by taking my hand and leading me back to the blanket. "Let's have a fire."

We collected some driftwood twigs and branches. I banked them against the log, then lit them. The sun was going down, and the day was turning chilly.

Sarah leaned against me. "I'm getting cold. Are you?"

"A little."

I took off my jacket and put it around her.

"What happened to you?" She must have felt the tape I still had wrapped around my ribs.

"I may have cracked a rib when some Sword of the Lord guys threw me out of the compound."

"They threw you out? You didn't tell me that. Have you seen a doctor?"

"No. It'll heal."

"You should see a doctor. You could have internal damage."

"Don't think so."

She then looked up at my face and what remained of the scrape as well as the bruise around my neck.

"More injuries from your investigation?"

"I wouldn't call them injuries."

She reached up and traced a scratch. I was touched. When she looked into my eyes and held my gaze, I kissed her. She put her arms around my neck and returned the kiss.

"That was nice," she said.

We kissed again, then she pushed me onto my back, got

on top of me and we made love on the blanket.

Well, we were on the blanket some of the time.

We laughed as we brushed off the sand.

"The kids will be home before long." She spoke with regret. It was getting dark.

She took my arm, creating an enchanted silence as we walked back to the car.

The next morning I called a florist and sent two dozen roses to Sarah's law office.

I included a note: "Last evening was wonderful! Hope it meant as much to you as it did to me. Your admirer, Jack."

An hour later she phoned.

"Thanks for the flowers. They're gorgeous. I don't want you to misunderstand though. What happened last night isn't going to be a regular occurrence."

"Of course. I knew that," I said.

20

Her brush-off had bruised my feelings. I wasn't used to being dumped. Or held at arm's length.

But then I reached the only sensible conclusion: I had a wonderful evening with a beautiful woman. What was there to be upset about?

Still…

I needed to think about something else. Get my mind off her. Get back to work on the investigation.

I had just pulled out on the road when I saw Mike's gray Silverado coming toward me. He slowed and rolled down his window.

"I saw you riding toward the river with Sarah yesterday. Hanging out with the hoity-toity?"

"We had a picnic."

"A little party along the river." Mike grinned. "She's a sharp woman. I'd like a piece of that."

I felt my temper flaring but controlled it. "You need to

grow up."

Mike only grinned wider, then gunned his engine and took off.

Mike was a good friend and his raunchiness when it came to women was not news to me, but sometimes...

I had managed to put the encounter behind me by the time I was entering the Recorder's Office. I asked to see the deeds for property in the vicinity of the marsh.

A few tracts were held by a trust, identified only by a number. The clerk said Missouri law allowed any further information to be kept confidential. Others were owned by county residents I didn't know. But I did know one, and that name reappeared on most of the properties: the developer Russell Collins.

Darlene lived in Marseille, so I called her. She invited me over.

A big-boned woman, she came to the door with a towel around her head. But she was unself-conscious about her appearance as, in an exuberant voice, she let me in into her rambling, brick, ranch-style home.

"I just got out of the shower. You got here fast."

She pooh-poohed my apology for rushing her, then led me to her kitchen table and offered coffee, which I accepted. I hadn't talked to her for some years, and she now was even more outgoing than when I'd seen her with my mother.

She had been married then; her husband, a financial adviser, had died several years ago. She was now selling real estate. I liked her manner and decided I'd know where to turn if I ever needed to buy or sell any property in Murray County.

"I appreciated your vote against the hog farm."

"Oh, I didn't like that. We don't need businesses that much."

"I was surprised that you were the only commissioner to oppose it. I thought several commissioners had been against it."

"They were, but they changed their positions."

"Do you know why?"

The question caused Darlene to pause. "I can only speculate. I imagine they changed their minds."

"There's talk, which I'm sure you've heard, that some of the votes may have been bought."

"Oh, I don't know if I'd give any credence to that. I had those thoughts myself. But when I mentioned my suspicions to a couple of others, they pooh-poohed that. The commission is more or less a good old boys club. I think that when Russ got Hal's support, the others saw which way the wind was blowing and lined up behind him. They usually do, you know. None of them wants to cross Hal."

"You're willing to do so."

"They make allowances for me, because I'm a woman. They don't like my independence but it doesn't surprise them. And as long as I'm just one dissenting vote I'm never any threat."

"How did Russ win over Hal? I heard he was neutral on the project at first."

"I don't know."

I waited for her to continue.

"Are you asking these questions for Sarah?"

"Yes."

"What does she hope to accomplish? The project has been approved."

"I guess you don't know. She's representing Charles Parker and she's trying to develop other suspects in the murder. Andre confronted Russ over rumors about a payoff, and she thinks that challenge may have had something to do with his death."

"That seems a stretch. I'm afraid I don't have any information that would help you. But if there are under-the-table deals, I'd like to stop them. I'm interested in honest government."

"So is Sarah."

"Tell her to stay in touch with me."

When I reported in to Sarah, I remarked: "I think Darlene might be an ally for you."

That didn't interest her. Instead, she was disappointed the interview hadn't produced more useful information.

"Another lead fizzles." She spoke grimly, making me feel that was my fault.

"But I've developed another one," she continued, her optimism rebounding. "I've learned whose account Max was transferring the funds to."

"Whose?"

"Minnie Hadley's, as you suspected."

"How did you find that out?"

"Because I want you to follow up on this, I'll tell you. But you must keep this to yourself."

"As you say."

"Max's account is with a bank corporation where my cousin is president. He didn't want to release the account name—that's confidential information under privacy rules—but I suggested that if he didn't help me the family might learn secrets he wouldn't want them to know."

She laughed. "Richie and I were close when we were growing up."

"Family blackmail?"

"You might put it that way. Richie was so mad he slammed the phone down on me. But he did mail me the name."

She said she'd tried to call Minnie in New Orleans, but the number was discontinued.

"I want you to find her address and fly down there and talk to her. Find out why that money was deposited in her account. Can you do that?"

"Yes. I've got some personal days coming. I assume you'll pay expenses?"

"Of course."

"I'll have to arrange for someone to cover for me at the bar."

"Okay. How soon can you go?"

"Maybe tomorrow morning."

"Do that, if you can," she said, hanging up.

21

The next afternoon, Tuesday, I dropped Buddy and Dusty off at Mike's and boarded a plane for New Orleans. When I was settled in at the Hotel Saint Philippe, on the west side of the French Quarter, it was too late to look for Minnie. On Bourbon Street partying tourists were milling in front of the loud and gaudy clubs. Most were depressed, wandering about looking for something they knew they wouldn't find.

Bright sunlight—and the gilded colorful facades of the Quarter's shops and homes—greeted me the next morning. Litter here and there on the uneven sidewalk was evidence of the partying the night before, but the streets were mostly vacant. Employees were sweeping up at one bar, and some shops were preparing to open. A woman wearing sunglasses exited a corner grocery/liquor store, which was covered with grillwork to keep out burglars. She looked like she had a hard night, and I recognized the smell of stale alcohol. An overweight older man in a white shirt, plaid shorts, white socks and black loafers walked his bulldog on the other, shady side of the street.

Minnie's home was in a lower-class neighborhood not far from the quarter. In response to my knock she opened the pink and robin's-egg-blue door a crack and peered through the opening.

When I identified myself, she hesitated, then opened the door. The wallpaper in the hall was faded but its floral pattern remained visible. I followed her to a cramped living room and sat down on her worn brown-striped sofa. Family photos, including one of a young Andre in a newsboy cap and T-shirt, were arranged around a celadon porcelain lamp on an end table.

Minnie seated herself in an armchair with impressive dignity. She was still a beautiful woman.

"I'm very sorry about Andre."

She began to cry. "I don't mean to cry. I can't help it."

She wiped her eyes with a handkerchief.

"Would you like a glass of sweet tea?"

"Yes. Thank you."

When she returned with the tea, I explained why I was there and told her about Max's bank book, showing her the images on his phone.

"We know the payments were made to you. Why did he send the money?"

She didn't answer at first. With bent arthritic fingers, she moved her glass on the coffee table. She kept her eyes down.

"Mr. Arnaud had been helping with Andre's expenses.

He sent money for school supplies and clothes. He paid for Andre's college too. We couldn't have afforded many of the things we had on my cleaning woman's salary. And Andre's father was no good. He never helped us at all."

"If you don't mind my asking, why did Max give you the money?"

She hesitated again, then said: "He was doing what his father told him to do. When Mr. Arnaud wasn't born yet, his father found out that I had to go live with my grandparents after my mother died, and he gave us money to help me out. Then when he died he said in his will that his son should continue to help support us."

I tried to not let my skepticism show. "That's an amazing story."

"It's because of what happened many years ago. That's when Antoine Arnaud fathered a child by a slave woman. She was my ancestor. The Arnauds have kept in touch with our family ever since."

She walked to a bureau and took out an old Bible from a drawer. The cover was loose at the binding and a corner was missing. Opening it carefully, she pointed to a family genealogy hand-written on a yellowed inside page.

I looked down the list. The birth and death dates for the last name were in the late 1800s.

"See. Here it shows Gabriel, born to Mabel—that's my ancestor—in 1841. It also says son of Antoine Arnaud. Then it says: Freed by Pierre Arnaud, 1858. Pierre was Antoine Arnaud's white son, and he and Gabriel were pals growing up.

When Pierre inherited the plantation in Little Dixie, he freed Gabriel and gave him money so he could learn the barbering trade and make a living."

"Did Andre know about the payments from Max?"

"No. I suppose Mr. Arnaud would have told him sometime. But Mr. Arnaud made me promise not to tell. He said he would stop sending the money if I ever told. So I never did. Until now I never told anyone."

"Have you thought about who might have killed your son?"

"I don't know who might have killed him. He was a good boy. I don't know why anyone would want to kill him."

I asked if Charles and Andre had been having any problems. She said no. "They got along real well."

She didn't know Kyle Hyde.

"You've been helpful," I said, then added sincerely: "Lots of people in Little Bend liked and respected your son. We're very sad about what's happened."

"Yes, sir. You're a good person. I don't believe Charles killed Andre. I hope you find out who did."

"We're doing our best."

22

I got home in the early hours of Thursday morning, slept late, then called Sarah. She was at the farm.

"The vet's here," she said. "I've got a horse with colic and can't talk right now. Why don't you come over and you can tell me what you found out? Do you ride?"

"I can stay on a horse if it's docile and well-trained."

"Let's go for a ride then. I was hoping to get in a ride this morning, and I have just the horse for you. We can talk on the trail."

I dug out a pair of boots and headed to her farm. When I drove up, Sarah was scattering grain by hand for a gathering of chickens, ducks and geese. I parked back so my truck wouldn't frighten them. As I approached her, a New Hampshire Red rooster lifted his head with its dangling comb and cocked it, giving me the eye. His multi-hued feathers shone in the sun.

I glared at him, which didn't bother him at all.

"Hi," Sarah said, only to be distracted when one of her dogs took after a goose. She ran after the dog and collared him.

"Bad dog, Oscar," she scolded. When she let him go, the shepherd mix sidled off, panting and looking pleased with himself.

"What did you find out?"

I relayed what Minnie had told me.

"That's not believable. You don't believe it, do you?"

"I'm doubtful, but..."

She paused for a moment, thinking.

"I'm sure the police would suspect that Max had a relation -ship with her. Or that she was blackmailing him. That could be the case. If he had a relationship with her, he wouldn't want that to become known. Or Minnie may have known some-thing else that Max couldn't afford to have become public."

"I can't see her as an extortionist."

"If her story is true, Max must have an extraordinary sense of family honor. He could stop making the payments and no one would be the wiser." She paused. "He could see the payments as an act of restorative justice. He is a Catholic."

"He isn't much of a Catholic. I've never heard of him going to confession or spending Sunday morning in church."

"It doesn't seem likely that he would have killed Andre unless blackmail was involved."

I followed her into the barn, where two horses were wait-ing in box stalls.

"That one's yours." She pointed to a bay mare who looked

at least 20 years old. "The tack is there. Can you saddle her?"

I managed, without embarrassing myself much. If Sarah had wanted to humiliate me she couldn't have found a better vehicle than horsemanship.

She led out her horse, a large dapple-gray warm blood. The gelding was eager to go, and she had to pull him back sharply to get him to mind. I managed to mount without falling off the other side of the mare. We walked the horses down a grass-covered lane leading to a pond in the distance. A field of rippling grasses rolled away to our left, and a smattering of cedars stood to our right.

"Let's canter," Sarah said, bending forward. The mare was a good follower and picked up her pace too. When we rounded a bend, we surprised a doe and her fawn at the edge of the field. With tails up, the deer high-stepped back into the woods.

The trail went through the forested side of the pond, and Sarah pulled the gray back to a walk, much to my relief. I ducked for a branch now and then as squirrels chattered angrily at us and several birds swooped by. I was following the flight of a noisy blue jay when a figure appeared to flit across the trail far ahead.

Sarah pulled up.

"You see somebody?"

"I thought so."

"No trespassing signs are posted along the property. No one should be here."

We stopped at a grassy knoll at the far side of the pond,

dismounted and sat in the grass, holding the horses' reins. I scrutinized the surroundings for any movement but saw nothing.

Three one-room cabins, which appeared to be rotting and about to fall down, stood in a row off to the side.

Sarah saw me looking at them. "Slave cabins. I'd tear them down but they have historical significance. Seeing them is always painful but I don't want to forget my family's history of slave-holding."

"You never owned a slave."

"That's true, but I'm enjoying the wealth those slaves created for my family. It's hard for me to come to terms with some of the things my ancestors did." She paused. "Andre's death has dredged up a family story I don't like to think about. I'd almost managed to forget it. My great-great-great grandfather had a servant boy castrated for watching his wife bathing.

"Can you imagine?"

"How did you learn about that?"

"My uncle told me. He wanted me to know my family's history, including its dark side."

She looked into the woods where we had come from, and I followed her gaze, wondering if she had seen something. But she was just looking into space. She turned to face me.

"I know racism persists in our unconscious attitudes, but I thought that the cruelty of terrorizing blacks was mostly in the past. With Andre's slaying, I wonder if it is. Think of police treatment of blacks. Maybe it's just retreated into the shadows."

She again got the far-away look in her eyes.

"I love this place. I came here regularly as a girl when my aunt and uncle lived here. My aunt and I would sit in a window seat, and she would read to me. She would pin up my hair. She made me feel beautiful, and I adored her. My uncle would tramp through the fields with me, helping me find insects for my collection. We loved it when a pheasant flew up and startled us, or a wild turkey strutted past."

Then she stopped herself. "But you're not interested in my reminiscences. Do you think Andre's death could have been a hate crime? Racism is a virulent disease."

"Yeah, I do. Though he could have been murdered because he was gay too."

"I know. There's just too many possible motives. This speculation isn't getting us anywhere. I guess we better get back."

When I ran into Cudinhead in town that afternoon, the constable had bad news for our case.

"Harriett Skidmore overheard Charles threaten to kill Andre after their quarrel." The Skidmores were neighbors of Charles. "That should lock it up."

"Funny she waited until now to tell you that."

"Oh, that's not unusual. People don't like to get involved."

The constable also said a hiker had found Andre's cell

phone along the Katy Trail and turned it in to the General Store.

"There's a blurry photo in it. But you can't see a face. Shank thinks Andre may have snapped the photo of his attacker."

"Does it look like Charles?"

"It could be him. I couldn't really say. It's a bad photo. We've sent it off to the lab to see what they can do with it. But we're not hoping for much."

"What about the dog tracks at the murder site?"

The constable looked down. "No one was sure the tracks had anything to do with the murder. Dogs are on the trail all the time, you know."

"Ralph said a dog attacked Andre on his bicycle."

"We didn't find that out until later."

"You didn't examine the tracks after you took Ralph's statement?"

"A dog track is a dog track. You can't learn much from that."

"What about that powder I gave you?" I was unable to quite conceal my contempt.

"The lab hasn't gotten back to us yet."

23

Max liked to say he was a lapsed Catholic. He'd laugh as though that were a good joke. Because of his religious heritage, however, he observed the major Christian holidays, which was why those of us at the restaurant were getting off at noon on that day, Good Friday. Max had been expected to show up but hadn't.

That didn't surprise us much—we assumed he'd been out partying the previous night. We did our jobs as expected but more efficiently than if he'd been there and with lighter spirits too.

I was last to leave. I had planned to spend the afternoon reading, but once home I kept thinking about Sarah. I left the laptop, moved to my piano and played "Tenderly," but my attention wandered from the notes. I knew what ailed me: I was love's captive.

"Bewitched, bothered and bewildered am I..." I picked out the melody on the keyboard.

Then my mind took one of those Pindaric drifts. Does anyone else my age know these songs? I wondered. I only knew them because my dad played them. Like me, he liked the piano. And nature.

Restless, I called Buddy and headed down to the dock and my boat despite a high wind and darkening clouds. A tugboat was pushing two barges upstream as I entered the channel, but I soon left them behind and was alone on the rolling river, that wild elemental force, the overpowering nature of which made me feel insignificant and restored my perspective. As so often on the river, the experience approached a religious one. I became calm and at peace and floated quietly for some time.

The current took me to a bend where a steamboat had sunk in 1856.

The River Queen had gone down with several of its passengers, and its remains still lay somewhere under the river. The vessel was undoubtedly covered in silt, if not buried in the river bottom. I peered into the dark water—you never know when the river might uncover one of its secrets.

But it was keeping this one.

I didn't want to end my reveries, but I knew I must.

I started the outboard, brought the boat about and motored to the entrance of the marsh and did my bird survey. I then headed out into the channel at trolling speed. I trained my binoculars on a stretch of sandy shoreline where I'd recently spotted an interior least tern, a rare experience. But she wasn't there today.

My thoughts turned again to Sarah. I told myself I had to

respect her wish to only have a casual relationship. I was lucky to have any relationship at all with her.

I was now approaching the spot where Andre's body had washed up. The place continued to have an almost magnetic power over me, and I yielded to its attraction, turning in to the bank. Buddy jumped off, excited about running and exploring sights and smells. The pawpaws were still exuding their rancid odor as I walked up the shore to the cottonwood where Andre's body had hung up. I glanced down at the towering tree's large and rough exposed roots, which looked like the arms of a tough and sinewy laborer.

I turned around to call Buddy but didn't see him.

"Buddy!" I shouted, expecting to see him tear out from the brush.

When he didn't, I looked around and saw dog tracks leading through rushes on a low-lying section of the shore. I followed them and saw Buddy nosing a log on top of the bank where the trail ran.

"Here boy." But the dog ignored me, so, annoyed now, I climbed up the bank, intending to grab him by the collar. Instead I stopped short. Buddy was sniffing, not a log, but another body. This one heavier-set but short and dressed in a charcoal-colored jogging outfit, with an arm that extended at an odd angle.

Walking around it to see the face, I was shocked to see

Max's vacant eyes.

When the officers arrived, the detective focused on me like a laser.

"Dead bodies seem to show up wherever you are. I suppose you don't know anything about this death either."

"No." He ignored my sarcastic tone.

Cudinhead looked on, studying me.

"You look like hell," he said, grudgingly. "I guess two bodies in a month is hard to take."

I said nothing. I didn't want his sympathy.

I hung around a while, watching the officers begin their investigation, then started toward my boat.

Shank stopped me.

"Don't leave town. We'll want to talk to you tomorrow." With emphasis, he added, "In the morning."

When I got home, I called Sarah and told her about Max.

She didn't say anything immediately. "Good grief. I didn't see that coming. It isn't another homicide, is it?"

"I don't know. I think it's probably an accident." I explained that Max apparently died from a fall.

I called Shank the next morning. "Should I bring an attorney?"

"That's up to you."

"Am I a suspect in a homicide investigation?"

"Everyone's a suspect right now."

I phoned Sarah and told her about the detective's summons. I told her I wanted an attorney with me. She said she'd meet me at the police station.

The two of us were ushered into an interview room, where the detective joined us.

"Where were you Thursday night?" Shank asked.

"I was at work." I looked over at Sarah, who met my glance but said nothing.

"Are there witnesses to verify that?"

"Sure. Lots of people were at the restaurant. I went home alone about 9:30. I was alone for the rest of the evening."

Shank dropped that line of questioning.

"Do you know why anyone might have wanted Arnaud dead?"

"No."

The interview took just over half an hour. Sarah had to leave for an appointment. "I'll call you later," she said as she walked away.

24

Angelica's face was drained of color and her eyes were dark from crying when she shuffled into work Monday. She looked as if she hadn't slept for days.

"You look terrible."

"I don't feel well."

"Why don't you go home?"

"I can't afford to lose my job."

"You won't lose your job. I'll tell Bernie you're ill." He was Arnaud's chef.

She gave me a teary but grateful look.

My phone rang after she'd left. It was Sarah.

"You're not the only one under suspicion in Max's death. Charles is also in trouble again. The police have picked him up for questioning."

"Why would they suspect him?"

"They didn't say."

"Does Charles have an alibi?"

"No. He was home alone that night. I was happy when he got out on bail. Now I wish he'd remained locked up."

"The police should have concluded that Max's death was an accident."

"You would think so. When you found Max's body, did you see anything to suggest otherwise?"

"Not really. An arm appeared broken, from the fall evidently. There were no other obvious injuries."

"When you have an opportunity, interview Tina. See if she knows anything about Max's payments to Minnie. Also, ask her if she knows why Max bailed out Charles. But be tactful. Remember her husband has just died. If you need to wait a while, do that.

"I'll tell Charles that Max put up his bail," she continued. "Now that Max's dead, I'm no longer bound by my pledge to secrecy. I'm hoping Charles can clear up at least this one mystery."

I was behind the bar when Tina walked in and took a stool.

"Double vodka. On the rocks with a twist of lemon.

I brought her the drink. "I'm sorry about Max."

She didn't bother to acknowledge my sympathy. "I need this," she said, lifting her glass. "I've just spent two hours at the sheriff's office, answering their damn questions. Those deputies have no manners at all."

"They interrogated you?"

"They gave me the third degree. They seemed to think I killed my husband. I weigh 105 pounds. How could I throw him off the bluff? I told them Max probably stumbled over the edge. He'd been drinking."

I was taken back by how coldly she talked about her husband. I concluded she wouldn't be offended if I questioned her about the night he died.

"Why'd he leave the house?"

"How do I know? Maybe he went running." She paused. "He may have gone out with someone. The doorbell rang, and then I heard Max talking to someone."

"Who?"

"I don't know. I was in the bedroom. Maybe Hal Weaver."

"Did you tell the police that?"

"No. They never asked. I could have told them other things too. But why should I help them?"

"What things?"

Tina looked warily at me but continued.

"An investigator from the state attorney general's office talked to Max about the hog farm decision. He said a commissioner was in on a deal. I wasn't very interested in local politics. Max was though. He thought Collins was up to something. Collins used to work for Max's dad, when Collins was a lawyer in St. Louis. Max swore that Murray County was crooked when his dad was alive, and it still was. It's all—disgusting!"

I wiped some spilled liquid from the bar top in front

of her.

"Max bailed Charles out of jail. Did you know that?"

"No."

"Do you know why he might have done that?"

"No." The topic didn't seem to interest her.

"He also had been making regular payments for years to Andre's mother? Did you know about those?"

"My husband didn't talk to me about his financial affairs." That seemed too glib an answer, but I couldn't tell whether I'd touched a nerve. She was a cool customer.

Tina had finished her drink. I made her another.

Then I phoned Sarah.

"The possible presence of Hal and the investigation by the attorney general's office is interesting," she said.

She had talked to Shank, who also had remarked on Tina's seeming lack of any grief.

"He said Tina had fallen asleep after Max went out and didn't realize until the next morning that he hadn't returned. She was apparently used to his going out and staying away. Or she didn't care enough to report him missing."

"If Max's death is a homicide, I'd mark her down as the prime suspect."

"Yes. Max had been cheating on her, and a woman can become enraged enough to kill a philandering husband."

But she added: "As we suspected, Shank told me he isn't convinced foul play was involved. He said the ground was scuffed up on the bluff above the body, but that could have happened if Max slipped and flailed about as he tried to regain his footing."

"In other words, we have another mystery."

25

Angelica rushed up to the bar the next afternoon, not long after arriving for work. Anguish distorted her face.

"The bitch fired me!"

"She can't do that for taking a day off."

"She didn't say why she did it. All she said was: 'You're fired as of now. Leave my restaurant and don't come back!' Her restaurant! It didn't take her long to move in after Max died."

"I'm sorry. Can you find another job?"

"In Little Bend? Get real!"

"I'm sorry," I said again. "If I can help let me know."

She was crying too much to talk now, and she turned and ran out.

Just before nine o'clock that evening, as I was closing down the bar, I got a call from Sarah. Her voice was tense but shaky.

"Jack, a truck nearly rammed us as we were driving home from Adrian's."

"What?"

"You heard me. It must have been that guy on the phone, or the guy who shot up Andre's apartment. The kids were terrified. He raced his truck up to our bumper as if he were about to hit us, then backed off. He did that three times. I was so relieved he drove on when I turned into the farm."

"Did you see who it was?"

"No, it was dark out, and he had his headlights on."

"Was it a black Dodge Ram again?"

"I have no idea. I couldn't see anything."

"Are you OK now?"

"Yes, but I still feel shaky." She wasn't talking to me like I was an immature younger man now. "I'm worried that he might return to the house here. We're all alone. Could you come over?"

"Sure. I'm just wrapping up here."

"Thank you. We'll feel so much better."

Ten minutes later I was on my way to her farm. In the light of my headlights the woods at each side of the road were dark and beautiful in their stillness. The trunks of the poplars stood out, shining gray-white, like tall luminaria. As I pulled up to her house, I noticed that every window was brightly lit.

When she let me in, she had a shotgun in one hand and a

fierce look on her face. Her four dogs were milling about her.

"Come in. Would you like a drink? We can go to the kitchen."

"I'll have whatever you're having. Is that gun loaded?"

"Yes, and I'm a good shot. I'm an experienced skeet shooter."

I laughed. "Well, I don't know that you need me here."

"Oh, I do. No one wants to be alone out here with two kids when someone dangerous is around. We'll have to modify your contract to include bodyguard duties."

"This is gratis."

"I'm reluctant to ask this, but could you stay the night? I can put you up in a guest bedroom?"

"Yes. There's nowhere I have to be."

"Thanks." She touched my arm to show her appreciation. "Do you have a gun with you?"

"Uh-uh."

She walked to a hall table, opened its drawer and took out a snub-nosed revolver.

"Here. Take this one and keep it with you."

I looked it over. It was a .32-caliber Smith and Wesson, not a big enough gun to stop a man. But I put it in my pocket to reassure her.

She moved to the liquor cabinet and poured a little Disaronno for each of us.

"Charles has invited us to his home Friday night for dinner. He wants to thank us for standing by him. He knows the risks we're taking and that our support isn't making us popular in Little Bend."

I made a wry smile.

"Can you go?"

"Yeah."

I then told her what Cudinhead had said. She hadn't heard about the cell phone photo. She said she'd ask Charles about the allegation that he threatened Andre.

Soon she left to prepare the guest bedroom. "It's the room on the right at the top of the stairs," she said when she came back down. "I hope you don't mind that I'm going to bed. I'm frazzled."

The comfortably furnished guest bedroom had its own bathroom, and the shower's hot water was relaxing. I wasn't too concerned about the truck driver. His actions—he did drive off—suggested to me that he only intended to intimidate Sarah again. Once in bed, I listened for a while to the sounds of the night. They were only the expected noises: an owl hooting, followed by the barking of a dog, and, somewhere in the distance, a car. Light from the moon coming through the side window cast a pale glow over the room and its furniture. Once the sound of the car receded, all was quiet, and I fell asleep.

Later, the creak of the bedroom door opening wakened me. The room was still dim but predawn light was coming through the window. I peered across the room, preparing to leap from the bed.

Then I realized Sarah had come in.

"Do you want some company?"

"I thought this wasn't going to be a regular occurrence."

"Do you really mind?"

"No."

She let the nightgown slip from her shoulders, lifted the covers and lay down next to me. I put my arms around her, and she snuggled up.

"You feel good…Strong."

As we made love, I felt passion I didn't know I had. Afterward I marveled that a woman so composed and self-controlled could be so natural and unself-conscious in bed.

And so sexy.

I fell asleep with my body entangled with hers. When I awoke, daylight was streaming in around the shade and Sarah was gone.

When I went downstairs, I heard Sarah and the children talking. I stopped before entering the kitchen to hear what they were saying.

"I think Daddy still loves you," I heard Emily say.

I heard Sarah sigh. "Eat your breakfast."

"Mom, do you like Jack?" Emily then asked.

"He's a very young man."

"He's tall."

"Yes, he's tall," Sarah said, laughing.

There was silence for a moment.

"Mom," Emily then said tentatively. "What's a homosexual?"

"It's someone who loves someone of the same sex."

"You mean like Charles and Andre."

"That's right."

"Why do they do that?"

"Well, you know how you may think a boy is cute. Some girls are different in that they think a girl is cute, or a boy thinks a boy is cute. That's just the way they're born."

"Oh." Then she said: "Most boys are gross."

I cleared my throat and walked into the kitchen in time to see Sarah smiling at Emily. George didn't appear to be paying any attention to the conversation. He was flying his spoon around his plate.

Sarah turned her smile to me. "Breakfast is ready."

When we'd finished eating, she walked with me to the door.

"Thanks for being my bodyguard." She gave me an intimate smile.

"I'll guard your body any time." I felt corny, but that didn't stop me. "Just give a whistle."

26

The next two days passed uneventfully. Sarah was preoccupied with other clients, and she didn't ask me to follow any new leads. I mulled over the two deaths and tried to connect the dots. But there were too few dots, or else my imagination wasn't fertile enough.

When I did talk to Sarah, she said Charles told her Harriett was lying when she claimed to have heard him threaten to kill Andre.

"Charles thought her husband put her up to that. He said Harvey dislikes him."

Friday evening, the night of the dinner, I met Sarah at the entrance to Charles' apartment. He came to the door wearing a food-stained apron.

"Welcome to my abode!"

As he ushered us in, he asked: "What's happening to this town? I thought it was as terrifying as it could get, but I was wrong."

"I now wake up wondering what shock we'll get today," Sarah said.

"But for one night let's forget this turmoil and enjoy the evening."

We moved to the dining room.

"Charles, how beautiful!" Sarah said as she took in the table adorned with china and heavy silver.

Charles led us to his "parlor," then handed each of us a champagne flute.

He raised his glass in a toast. "To true friends!"

"This is a super cocktail. What's in it?" I was thinking Arnaud's might want to offer it at the bar.

"Champagne and Pernod. "It's called 'Death in the Afternoon.' After the Hemingway novel. The death theme seemed appropriate."

His mood suddenly lightened and he began to regale us with his jail experiences.

"It's a scary place. I can't tell you how scary. Some of those guys are mean enough to fry a puppy. I never acted more straight. Take my word for it, you don't want to spend any time in that jail. The food was appalling. It makes you long for the Pancake House. And the fashion, well, orange doesn't go with my skin tone!"

Sarah and I were laughing, but Charles suddenly turned melancholy and serious.

"I hope I don't have to go back."

Despite Sarah's earlier suggestion, Charles turned the conversation to the investigations.

"Did the prosecutor say anything after the interview? I thought my grilling would never end. I can't believe the police think I killed Max. That's even more absurd than the charge in Andre's death. Why would I kill Max?"

"I don't think they're zeroing in on you," Sarah said. "They've interviewed several people."

"Including me," I inserted. "And they'll most likely conclude his death was accidental."

"I heard that someone found Andre's cell phone and that he snapped a photo of whoever attacked him," Charles said. "Is that true?"

"Yes," Sarah said.

"Can't they see it's not me?"

"Unfortunately not. All that's showing is a raised arm and a blurry partial figure."

"Well, I hope the police find the killer and leave us alone. But enough talk about the men in blue. They're only attractive in the movies!"

He glanced at me, apparently thinking his witticism might have shocked me.

"By the way," he said, "I know what Andre had on Russ. He saw Russ with another man in a gay bar in St. Louis. A friend told me."

He looked meaningfully at us for a moment and then leaned forward on his antique loveseat and began to talk about the "Missouri" dinner he'd prepared.

"I was inspired by a dinner Andre and I had at the marvelous Kansas City restaurant Tallgrass. I don't follow recipes. I prefer to experiment. The appetizers will be miniature catfish cakes, from wild fish caught locally." Charles beamed as he said this. Sarah had told me he considered himself a foodie.

"Fabulous!" Sarah said.

"Places at the table everyone!" Charles commanded. "Sit."

Once we had eaten the first course, and Charles had demanded our opinion of it—even I overcame my reserve and gave it a big thumbs-up—he went through the swinging door to his kitchen and returned with a tray of bowls.

"Big Sky soup. The drippings of red pepper sauce on this corn and cream concoction resemble a prairie sunset!"

Three other courses, with wine pairings, followed: a watercress salad, duck confit with wild mushroom sauce, and Ozarks pudding.

After the dessert, we returned to his parlor for port.

Charles now dropped his effort to be entertaining. "I can't stop thinking about death. The more I think about it the more sick at heart I become. I can't sleep."

"Sleep problems are normal during a time of grieving," Sarah said sympathetically, "but…"

Charles interrupted her.

"A psychologist might say so. But I'm in despair, and it's more than emotional. It's intellectual. It's in my soul."

He looked at Sarah, appearing to have forgotten that I was in the room.

"Why did Andre have to die so young?" His pain distorted his features. "Why should I be chosen to go on living?"

"Those are questions for theology. Why don't you talk to Margot? She's a knowledgeable minister."

"Theology!" Charles said disdainfully. "You may take consolation in a clergyman's assurances, but I can't. Theology is just convoluted nonsense to dispel doubts people have about religion."

Sarah fell silent.

"You could go out with me on the river tomorrow?" I was attempting to return the conversation to a more comfortable place. "Nature can be good medicine..."

"That bit about nature is a Romantic viewpoint," Charles interrupted, sighing. "I don't do nature."

He turned away, looking immensely sad.

"No one—not ministers, theologians or poets—face the awful truth. Reality's unspeakably cruel. If there's a God, he's evil. What else can you think when the poorest countries suffer such demonic crimes and horrific disasters? When so many innocent children are bombed or suffer abuse and starve? When women undergo sexual mutilation or are stoned for adultery or burned alive?"

Charles' face revealed his agony.

"How else can anyone explain why Andre, gentle Andre, died so cruelly?"

Charles dropped his head into his hands, crying so deeply his shoulders shook. After a moment he raised an arm and waved his guests away.

"Go home!"

27

From the glow through my window shade, I believed dawn had arrived but the digital clock displayed 2:23 a.m. I jumped out of bed and raised the shade to an other-worldly sight. The night was light, like a mellow summer evening, and black smoke billowed skyward, twisting into the shapes of monsters like a child's nightmare.

I dressed and hurried to my truck.

Others were driving to the fire too. Sirens wailed and beams from the flashing lights of squad cars and fire trucks swirled through the night like Star Wars light swords. When I reached the town's center, I could see flames shooting up from Artful Antiques' roof. A crowd had collected on the streets to watch firefighters directing streams of water onto the building.

A man with a beard lurking near the back of the crowd caught my eye. I observed the silhouetted figure until it faded into the smoky haze.

A terrible possibility gripped me: Had Charles stayed up

drinking and, in his despair, set fire to his own house, perhaps in an attempt to commit suicide?

But Charles was alive, huddled in his bathrobe outside his home's entrance, conferring with the fire chief. He pointed to the sidewalk. I moved in and read the crude red letters on the concrete: "HOMO GET OUT."

As the crew suppressed the fire, the night's darkness began to return.

I joined Charles, who stood forlorn, gazing at his smoking building.

"I've lost everything. Do you know the effort that went into collecting those pieces? Many are irreplaceable."

"Were you able to save your personal things?"

"Nothing. Not one possession. I was lucky to get out alive. The smoke woke me."

"Where are you going to stay?"

"Sarah's coming to get me. I'm done with this town."

With the fire under control, I went home. Unable to sleep, I read from Shelby Foote's history of the Civil War until daylight. When I shuffled into the kitchen at 8 o'clock, I discovered I was out of coffee.

I groaned. "Just my luck."

I needed other groceries as well so I headed to the General Store. Over the scanner came the voices of firefighters relaying messages as they wrapped up at the fire scene. On Main

Street the smell of smoke lingered. Police tape cordoned off the blackened shell of the antiques store, which still smoldered.

When I entered the store, I was surprised to find a dozen or so townspeople inside.

"…I heard Parker was having financial problems," Harvey was saying. "I think he started the fire himself to get insurance money."

Don Hart, the postmaster, disputed that. "You're forgetting what was painted on the sidewalk."

"He wrote that to throw suspicion away from himself," Harvey countered. "If he gets off on the murder charge, he'll be set. He'll have what Hadley left him and the insurance money. We'd never have had this trouble if these guys hadn't moved into town. We've never had crime like this before."

"The town owes a debt to Charles and Andre," I said. "They brought in business. And favorable publicity."

Harvey looked scornful. "We'd be better off without these city people."

"That's not true," I asserted. "Look at what the Nelsons have done for this town. Look at what Sarah has done."

My defense of Sarah stirred Harvey's ire.

"What has she done besides try to stop the hog farm? If she succeeds in blocking it, I expect her dad will buy up the land. She thinks we're hicks who don't know anything."

"You've got her wrong," I said.

Eric looked over at me, signaling agreement with a smile. But I was disgusted with myself for arguing with a fool.

The conversation returned to the fire.

"One thing's sure, the fire was no accident," Billy Finlay, the service station's owner, said.

An older widow, Ruth Martin, concurred. "That's true. But I don't think Charles did it. Whoever did the murders probably set his store on fire too."

"He did the murders," Harvey exclaimed in exasperation.

A young housewife, Diane Barker, spoke up. "I don't believe that. I think someone set the fire to drive him out of town."

"We'll know more when the fire marshal completes his investigation," Eric said. "Until then this is just talk."

His remark discouraged more opining and everyone began moving on.

28

Sarah phoned Monday morning to alert me to a court hearing that forenoon in her request for an injunction to stop the hog farm.

"Come, if you want. It might be interesting. And you know Russ will be there."

When I walked into the district courthouse in Jefferson City, Sarah was sitting very upright in her chair behind the plaintiff's table. In her black suit and white blouse she looked the image of television's idea of the professional woman lawyer. I knew she was doubtful about her chances to prevail but she was putting on an optimistic front.

The defendants' table was unoccupied although the hearing was scheduled to start in five minutes.

Then the court clerk broke in. "All arise for the Honorable Margaret Faulkner." From the back door the judge, a dowdy-looking woman in a black robe, walked in and seated herself behind the bench.

"Court is now in session. I see the plaintiffs' counsel. Where is the counsel for the defense? Clerk, please check the hallway."

The white-haired clerk walked spryly out into the hall then returned.

"There's no one there, your honor."

"We'll give them a few more minutes." She and the clerk chatted.

"Go check the hall again, Clarence," she said after about 15 minutes. "And if no one is there, call their office."

The clerk walked out again.

"Still no one there, your honor," he said when he returned. "And the phone call went to voice mail."

The judge looked stern. "The defense having failed to appear, the court rules in favor of the plaintiffs." She banged her gavel loudly.

Sarah was elated. "I can hardly believe this!"

She picked up her briefcase.

"Let's go into the hall. I want to make some phone calls to let others in on the news."

I waited in the background, watching her animated end of the conversations. When she shut down her phone, she smiled at me.

But then the smile faded. "I wonder why they dropped their project."

"Good question. Do you think Russ feared attracting more attention to it? If there were underhanded deals, he might not have wanted attorneys sniffing into it."

"Hmm. That could be one explanation."

We walked together out of the courthouse. "I've a favor to ask. Clark, my ex, is coming through town and wants to meet me for lunch. I don't want to be alone with him. I want to keep this meeting on an impersonal level. Would you join us?"

"Sure. Consider it bodyguard duty."

Her response was a smile.

Adrian's, the only café in Little Bend, had a deli and bakery and served family-style meals. When we entered, her ex-husband hadn't arrived yet. We took the table in the front by the window, and Sarah ordered a glass of chardonnay.

She was sipping the wine when Clark's BMW cruised in. He was cocky as he got out of the car. His upscale clothes—a short-sleeve print shirt, linen slacks and a baseball cap—made him look out of place in Little Bend.

He took off his designer sunglasses as he entered. "Nice place."

He sat down across from Sarah and surveyed the café's brick interior walls, bentwood chairs and old-fashioned glass-front counter. When he took off his cap and put it on the table, I noted the Brooks Brothers insignia. Sarah introduced us.

He didn't try to disguise his annoyance at my presence.

We chatted about his trip to Little Bend and the weather. He was facile at small talk—and charming. Too charming.

"How's your job going?" Sarah asked.

"Business is great. I expect to be made partner soon."

He asked how the children were doing.

"They're fine."

He talked as if the two of them were alone. Apparently my presence was insignificant.

"Do you think we made a mistake?" he asked.

"No."

"I know you're not happy."

I could see that comment galled her.

"You can't be happy without a real family."

She laughed rudely. "I'm quite happy, thank you."

"What about the kids?"

"What about them?"

"They'd be better off if the family was together again."

"They would not."

Clark fell silent. He ate the last of his chicken breast sandwich, swallowed the rest of his wine and stared out the window.

"Well, think about it."

When he was gone, she turned to me. "I'll think about murdering him."

29

The emergency community meeting drew a crowd to the First Christian Church basement. People filled the chairs and stood against the walls. Even the town crank, Claud Koster, had shown up, though he was off by himself in a corner.

Sarah walked over.

"Where's Charles?" I asked. He had moved in with Sarah the night of the fire.

"He wasn't up to coming. I almost didn't come myself. I'm nervous now about driving at night."

The mayor brought the meeting to order.

"Listen up, everyone!" Eric waited for the hubbub to subside. "What this community has been through in the past few weeks has been shocking and disturbing. I called this meeting so you could hear what the police are doing, and so that we can listen to your ideas about further steps we can take. I'll turn the floor over now to Detective Rod Shank of the Murray County Sheriff's Office."

The detective came to the front and, in a strong voice, reported on the progress of the investigations into the deaths of Andre and Max.

"We've filed charges against Charles Parker for the murder of Andre Hadley, and we think we have a good case. We're still investigating Max Arnaud's death and questioning persons of interest. But his death may not involve foul play. We think it was accidental. He probably died from a fall from the bluff."

Shank also said that the fire inspector was investigating the Artful Antiques fire.

"Preliminary evidence suggests the fire is arson, but it's too early for a determination."

The detective noted that the TIPS hotline was offering a $1,500 reward for information leading to the arrest of a suspect in the fire or for important leads in the deaths.

"All these incidents may be connected and the work of a single individual or they may be unrelated. We're doing our best to find answers, and we'll do everything in our power to apprehend those responsible."

Don stood up.

"I don't think you're getting to the bottom of these crimes," the postmaster said. "What makes you think Charles killed Andre? Have you questioned that survivalist clan? You need to check them out. They're up to no good."

There was a murmur of agreement from the crowd.

"I can't go into detail," the detective said, "but we have physical and other evidence to believe as we do. And we have no reason to disturb a peaceful religious group, no matter how unpopular they are."

When no one else said anything, Eric turned to Harry.

"Harry, you have an announcement you want to make?"

"Yes." Harry stood up self-consciously and brushed a hand over his flattop. "We all appreciate that the police are doing their best to protect us and solve these crimes. But we need to pitch in to keep this community safe. I talked to the sheriff and he told me to go ahead" (he stopped to nod at Shank and get his concurrence) "so I'm starting a neighborhood watch. We want residents out driving around town and looking out for trouble 24 hours a day. I'll be sitting at the table in the back with a sign-up sheet. I have a map of the community, and I'm looking for captains for districts that I marked out."

The mayor then opened the meeting to comments from the floor.

"We should keep an eye on the children," Cheryl said. "I urge all parents to know where their children are at all times and keep them inside after dark."

Harvey then spoke up. "Most people around here have guns. We need to keep them loaded and ready. That's what I'm doing with mine."

That prompted the constable to rise.

"It's fine to have a gun for self-defense." Cudinhead was breathing a little heavily. "But everyone needs to follow safe procedures. Don't keep your gun loaded, and be careful with it. We don't want children or neighbors caught up in accidental shootings.

"You could all be more helpful by watching for people who don't belong here, or anything unusual or suspicious. Call me or the sheriff's department if you see anything like that. Don't worry if what you report turns out to be nothing. We're happy to check out everything. You never know when your tip may solve these cases."

Margot stood up. "I'm holding a community candlelight service upstairs following this meeting," the minister said. "All of you are invited, whatever your faith. We can all take comfort from knowing that we are facing this together."

The next day I attended the memorial service for Max in Columbia. The funeral chapel was packed with mourners. His neighbors and customers had liked him. Afterwards, I drove into Little Bend on my way home. Mike was patrolling for the neighborhood watch.

I stopped and rolled down my window.

"Anything happening?"

"Not much. Billy was hanging around the Nelsons' yard. He was up to no good, I'm sure of that. Their dog was barking at him. I'd bet that druggie was trying to steal the dog."

I knew dog fighters sometimes took family pets to use as sparring partners for their pitbulls to get them used to killing their opponents. I didn't like to think of the Nelsons' Scottish terrier meeting that bloody fate.

"When Billy saw me he got in his truck and tore off."

I drove on to the General Store and got out to read the announcements taped on its windows. One was a poster on a party at the theater to celebrate Andre's life.

I phoned Sarah.

"Is the celebration for Andre your idea?"

"Guilty as charged. But Kelly Morgan is organizing it. We're actually doing it to raise money for Charles, but, because of the charges against him, we're saying the money will go to help Artful Antiques recover from the fire. The fire insurance won't cover Charles' costs so, on top of his legal trouble, he has more money problems than ever. Kelly said no one at the theater thinks he's guilty and they're all his friends. They'd like to help him."

"It's a great idea."

"The best part of it is that Charles will be able to be there. It was really hard for him to miss the funeral."

"How's his state of mind?"

"He's been down. Today he stayed in his sweats and hardly left his room. I tried to get him to go pet the horses or go for a walk around the property, but, you know him, he says he doesn't 'do outdoors.' I gave him my volume of Auden's poetry, and he's reading that.

"But, you know, he continues to be in complete denial about the fire. He doesn't want to talk about it. He said this morning he's thinking about opening his store somewhere else, maybe Kansas City."

"I'd hate to see him take his store out of town."

"I know. The store is an asset that makes Little Bend unique. I'm hoping the party will make him feel better about the town again and change his mind about moving."

Neither of us had any inkling then that Charles wouldn't be enjoying the event for Andre this time either.

30

The next afternoon Ted was back at the bar, still down in the dumps about Mildred.

"Still haven't heard from her?"

"Not a word. I don't even know where she is. She could be in Mexico for all I know."

The salesman was my only customer. As usual, he was also the first of the day. I was looking out the window at the parking lot when a silver Boxster convertible rolled in and Tina stepped out. I hardly recognized her. She wore white sunglasses and a red sheath dress. She surveyed the property, then walked toward the front doors with a swing in her stride.

She passed by me. "Come see me."

When I entered the office, Tina sat in her husband's leather wing chair behind the ponderous oak desk. Her eyes were appraising as they focused on me.

"Bernie is going to temporarily run the restaurant for me. I'll be hiring a permanent manager but in the meantime I want you to assist Bernie any way you can. You can manage the beverage end of things, can't you?"

"Yes."

"I've got some things I need to do out of town so I won't be here for a while."

Her body language indicated the meeting was over. So I left.

I was standing by the hostess's desk a few minutes later when Tina approached me again.

"Kelly asked us to donate the liquor and provide bar staff for the theater party a week from Friday night. Can you work the event and arrange for whatever help you'll need?"

I nodded.

Tina began to walk out then stopped and turned back. "Thanks for telling police there was a man with Max the night he died. Got me off their list and free to go."

She then swirled and walked into the dining room. A younger man in a golf shirt and sport coat stood up from a table and joined her, and together they strolled out to the Porsche. He opened the passenger door for her then got in the driver's seat.

The shiny new convertible roared away much faster than it had arrived.

Later that evening, Sarah stopped by the bar. She looked tense as she ordered her drink.

"A martini."

"What's up?"

"That guy called again, and he was more threatening this time. He said: 'You don't take a hint, do you? Do you want to get hurt? If you keep nosing around and defending that homo, that's what's going to happen.' Then when I was on my way home, he followed me in his pickup. He pulled alongside at a stop sign, rolled down his window and shouted, 'I meant what I said. I can get to you at any time.' I'm getting scared."

"You should be. What did he look like?"

"He was a big guy with a shaved head."

"And the truck? Can you describe it?"

"Only that it was black and large. I took a photo with my phone as it roared away."

"Can I see the photo?"

She showed it to me. It was a Dodge Ram 3500.

"It looks like the same truck I saw outside Andre's place."

We looked at each other for a moment.

"You need to take precautions."

"I have. I called Shank to report what happened and sent him the photo. He said he'd have deputies drive by my home frequently. I also gave him part of the truck's license number—CYV 11. That was all I could make out. I purchased some mace too and bullets for my pistol. I'm now keeping the gun and the mace in my purse."

"Do you want me to resume my bodyguard duties?"

"Actually, yes. Would you? Charles is at the house, but I'll feel safer if you are there too."

"I'll pack up a suitcase and come over tonight. Buddy can stay again at Mike's."

"Bring some things for a trip to Kansas City too. I have to drive there for a corporate board meeting next week. I want you to come along. We can stay at the company condo. Can you do that?"

"Do you think there might be another irregular occurrence?"

"That would be up to you." She smiled.

31

Thursday was quiet. But on Friday morning the prosecutor's office dropped a bombshell: It charged Charles with murdering Max too.

Sarah was dumbfounded.

A squad car came to her farm to re-arrest Charles and return him to jail. Seeing Charles sitting in the back of the police car, tears streaming down his face, was hard for Sarah to take.

"Are they trying to make the poor man crazy?" she asked. "Let's go see Bill."

I had started to go everywhere with her now during my off hours.

"What in the world are you thinking?" she asked the prosecutor.

"Our investigations have turned up some new information," he said. "When we subpoenaed Max's bank records, we discovered he'd been making payments to Andre's mother for years."

"There's an explanation for those payments, though I don't know whether to believe it," Sarah interjected. "Minnie said Max made them because Andre and Max were distantly related. One of the early Arnauds in this area had fathered a child by a slave who was Minnie's ancestor."

When I heard that explanation out loud, I thought it sounded crazy. Bill did too.

"Don't tell me you buy that."

Sarah held her tongue.

"I don't buy that story. She's either covering up for her son, or Max told her that so she wouldn't be suspicious of the payments. Andre wanted the money to go to her so the payments wouldn't be traced to him."

"What do you think Andre had on Max?" Sarah asked.

"We don't know yet but we'll find out. Max and Andre both lived in New Orleans when the payments began. It's probably something that happened down there."

"OK. Let's assume your theory is correct. Why do you believe Charles is connected to Max's death?"

"The fact that Max bailed Charles out of jail. You might have told me about that, by the way." Sarah ignored that remark. "We think Charles blackmailed Max into putting up the bond and that he was now getting the regular extortion payments."

The prosecutor didn't stop for an answer.

"We believe Max finally had had enough with the blackmail and told Charles he wasn't paying any more and was going to expose the scheme. They got into a struggle and Charles overpowered him and pushed him off the bluff.

"Charles can't explain where he was that night," Bill continued, "and one of Max's neighbors said she saw a person fitting Charles' description leaving the trail that night. She has identified Charles in a line-up."

"Line-ups and witnesses, especially when the sightings happen at night, are often unreliable," Sarah said. "Your theory's a stretch."

Once back in her car, she dropped her head to her hand. "If Charles' defense was difficult before, it's now much tougher."

But a moment later she rallied. "We'll have to cast doubt on the so-called evidence. Without the witness, Bill has nothing. Either that, or find the killer—if there was one. Most likely, the death was a mishap."

We drove to the jail and spent an hour with Charles, trying to calm him. The new charges were causing him to come unraveled again.

"What fiction will they think up now?" he moaned. "They have more imagination than Hollywood."

32

Trying to absorb the latest developments was messing with my mind, so I turned to a more straight-forward crime: my home burglary. I had my suspicions but needed proof. On Monday I phoned Cudinhead.

"Any results on the powder left in my kitchen?"

"It was meth."

"Fingerprints?"

"The lab couldn't lift any prints."

"What do you make of it? The packet could have been planted."

"Nah," the constable said, "the intruder just dropped it. He was careless. Stupid, like most burglars."

A convenient conclusion, I thought, but perhaps correct.

That afternoon a General Assembly committee was

conducting a hearing on legislation to declare a year-long moratorium on development along the length of the Missouri running through Murray County. The moratorium would allow time for completion of the environmental study. Knowing of my participation in the study and my interest in preserving natural habitat along the river, Rep. Clyde Bauman, the House's leading conservationist, had asked me to testify.

The drive through the rolling hills was spectacular. Soon the dome of the state Capitol came into view. The imposing marble government building, set atop a bluff with a splendid panorama of the Missouri River, gleamed almost white in the sunlight as I pulled my truck into a parking area.

I walked past the statue of Thomas Jefferson and up the Capitol's broad steps.

Inside the towering bronze entrance doors, my footsteps were the only ones resonating in the hall and on the grand staircase. I went on to the hearing room where the House Committee on Tourism and Natural Resources was meeting. Only a handful of people had collected in the public seating area, though the session was to be called to order in a few minutes. I imagined that most of them, like myself, were there to testify on the legislation. Among them was Hal Weaver.

The committee member attendance was sparse too.

Bauman strolled over. "It's too nice a day to be in here. Thanks for testifying. I know you appreciate the beauty of the river, especially down from Little Bend. I'd like to think my grandchildren will be able to enjoy those views someday."

The banging of the gavel by the committee chairman interrupted our conversation. I was the third speaker, after a landowner and a representative of the Nature Conservancy. When it was my turn and I read my remarks, most of the lawmakers weren't listening. Instead they reviewed their notes or chatted with staff members.

"Any questions?" I asked when finished. When no one said anything, I asked that my statement be included in the committee minutes.

Hal testified as I expected, arguing that riverside development would spur growth of the regional economy.

When I got back to Columbia, I drove to Sarah's office, then followed her back to her place. I volunteered to make dinner, an offer she took me up on.

"Take whatever you need from the refrigerator," she said.

I thawed some ground beef in the microwave, got out some canned tomatoes and kidney beans, and threw together one of my standbys: chili.

"You're not exactly a gourmet cook, are you?" she said when I announced that the meal was ready.

I shrugged. What could I say? But my feelings were hurt. I was proud of my chili.

33

The next morning, Sarah and I left for her board meeting in Kansas City. Mike was again taking care of my pets and Cheryl was babysitting the kids. It was a monotonous drive until we arrived at the long hill on I-70 that looked down across the city from its most flattering entrance.

I drove to the Country Club Plaza. The company condo was on the top floor of a modern glass-and-steel building rising above the ritzy shopping area. Inside, the condo had blond wood interior walls and floors and minimalist furniture. Some might have found the condo cold and impersonal, but I liked it.

It was nearing lunchtime when we were settled in.

"Let's go to the club," Sarah said. "We can get lunch there and avoid the hassle on the Plaza."

The venerable private horse club, Boot and Spur, nestled in ample acreage in a leafy suburb. Stone pillars marked its entrance, and, after turning in, its gentrified atmosphere made it a world apart. Two helmeted women on tall bay horses were walking them out to a paddock, past a groom carrying a bucket to the stables.

We entered through the double doors of the stone clubhouse and walked through a lobby with a silver-laden Western saddle on display. Sarah led the way into a hall.

"Dad will be joining us," she said as we entered the dining room. He hadn't arrived yet, however, so we took a table and ordered our drinks.

"Nice place," I said.

"I more or less grew up at this club," Sarah said. "I was on the swim and dive teams, and I learned to play tennis, shoot and ride here. I sometimes think I should be providing an amenity like this for George and Emily."

"In Little Bend they can run free and be natural kids. There's a lot to say for that."

She became nostalgic.

"So many memories are associated with this place for me. On fall trail rides, with a chuck wagon in tow, we rode our horses over mile after mile of Kansas' Flint hills. The prairie always seemed as endless as the swelling waves of the ocean. Few things were as sweet as watching the sparks fly up when we gathered around the campfire in the darkness. It was so empty out there. There were no city lights at the horizon, no sign of civilization."

"That sounds wonderful."

"It was. But other things were embarrassing. Some members came to parties in black face and corn rows. A so-called winter trail ride took us all to a Plaza hotel where there was partying. And lots of liquor. Some of the younger wives usually ended up dancing on tables. That was a lot of fun. Until it got out of hand."

We heard her father's booming voice before we saw him.

"Don't tell him about the truck driver," she said as he walked through the doorway. "I don't want to worry him. Fatherhood to him means being my protector, and he takes that duty seriously."

He came up and gave her a kiss on the cheek. "I'm glad we could fit a lunch in. You look beautiful as always."

"It's always good to see you, Dad."

"You've been showing up again in *The Star*. How's the murder defense going?"

"I'm still trying to develop suspects. We're investigating several people, and we've got some promising leads."

"The defendant—what's his name? Parker?—is a lucky guy to have you defending him."

"I hope I don't let him down. Charles is a friend and so was Andre. I still can hardly believe Andre was murdered. And Charles is now charged in Max's death. I imagine you know about his fatal 'fall.'"

"Yes. I was sorry to hear that. He was a likable guy. Not a likely murderer."

"Whatever is behind this violence, I'm suspicious of Russ Collins, the hog farm developer, or Hunthausen, the leader of a religious cult. Maybe you've heard of it."

Her dad nodded.

"I think politics could have been behind Andre's slaying. I wouldn't rule out Hal Weaver, the presiding county commissioner, either."

"I think you're letting your imagination carry you away," her father said. "The presiding county commissioner's not going to get involved in a crime like this. It's probably some wacko."

We stopped to order lunch. Her dad and I had the Kansas City strip steak and Sarah asked for the salmon salad. After the server came with our lunches, we dined quietly for a while.

"I've considered moving back to Kansas City," Sarah said eventually. "I've tried to make a home in Murray County, but this violence disturbs me. I don't know whether I'll ever belong there."

"I wondered if the country life would suit you," her dad said. "You were a rising star in the legal community here. You don't have the same opportunities in Columbia."

Sarah didn't quite agree. "My professional life is pleasant there, more enjoyable than in Kansas City. And Charles' case is the most challenging I've worked on."

"Don't you miss your friends though and the, let's say, diversions of the city?"

"I love the farm and its solitude. But sometimes, I'll admit, its peacefulness and bucolic setting aren't enough. Life can become too relaxed. Boring. And maybe the kids would be better off in school here. Some of the children in the local school can be rough. Then I think about St. Francis

Day School and my well-behaved friends and kind teachers."

"Your mom and I have been concerned about George and Emily." Her dad looked at her over his half glasses. "We don't want to interfere in your life, but we do think they'd be better off in Kansas City. We'd like you to move back here where we could be involved in their lives and help you with them."

Sarah toyed with her salad.

"You know that I've also been concerned that the situation there is dangerous for you," her dad continued. "I wish you weren't involved in the murder cases. I thought you should have stayed away from the factory farm controversy too. You need to tread carefully. Who knows what kind of people you might scare up out of the brush. I know you won't be deterred but this worries me. I'm worried for your safety."

"I know, Dad. I'll take every precaution. Jack is acting as my bodyguard."

He turned to me. "Good. Keep an eye on her."

To Sarah he said: "Why don't you get away awhile? You could go to the villa or the condo. They're available." Sarah had told me that the family had a condo in Florida and a villa in Italy. "You look like you could use some rest and relaxation."

Sarah just raised her eyebrows.

"I'll see you at the board meeting," he then said to her, giving her another peck on the cheek as he left.

I drove Sarah later that afternoon to the meeting at the development company's headquarters in an historic building downtown within sight of the Missouri River. The meeting lasted more than two hours, during which time I waited in the lobby and read a book on my phone. Sarah was chatting with two men in suits as she came back down in the elevator.

She was preoccupied as we walked to her car.

"We have things to talk about." She didn't say what they were.

34

That afternoon Sarah said she wanted to show me something. She took me to a construction site on 47th Street on the Plaza less than a half mile from the condo. A partially completed high-rise there took up most of the block.

"This is our biggest current project," she said, referring to the family company. "We've got a national accounting firm signed up as the primary tenant. But the work's not going well. Change orders are causing costs to balloon. We think those costs are covered under the original contract. But the contractor refuses to finish the work unless we modify it. So the project sits here half-finished. There's been no progress for six months.

"The recession was already hurting us, like most other developers of commercial, and this snafu isn't helping."

"Why did you show me this?"

"I think you'll know soon."

We strolled back on 47th Street into the heart of the Plaza, doing some people watching and window gazing. Then we went to dinner at a small French restaurant in Brookside, a sedate neighborhood of bungalows and other older homes. The food was superb, and we lingered with our wine until we were alone.

I was beginning to like this bodyguard role.

When we went back to the condo for the night, I thought she might invite me into her room. But maybe to forestall an overture from me, she said she was tired then went to bed alone.

The next morning she came out of her room in her robe, looking more than fetching. She carried a file of papers and placed them on the kitchen island.

"You might want to look at these. They are records indicating that Jennings Development Corp. has land holdings in Murray County. I can't determine from these papers precisely where the land is. If I inquire into details, that always annoys Dad, so I'm not asking him."

While she showered and dressed, I perused the records. When she returned to the kitchen, I asked about her interest in the holdings.

"I didn't know we had any in Murray County. Dad is a hands-on guy and is aware of most of what the corporation is up to. I wonder how much he knows about the county. Maybe he knows more than he's let on and that's why he thinks I may be in danger."

"Can't we find out where these properties are?"

"I don't want to pry into Dad's business affairs."

"Do you mind if I look into them?"

"I suppose that's OK. I want to stop at the house and talk to Mom. Rebecca will make us breakfast, and then we can go back to Little Bend."

The Jennings home was an early 20th Century Italianate mansion topping a hill in several acres a block off Ward Parkway, the city's premier boulevard. A tall wrought-iron fence surrounded the property, and we entered through an electric gate and up a long, concrete driveway to a circle drive in front of the home's entrance.

The front door opened onto a wide central hallway with a black and white tile floor. I followed Sarah into a dining room with mahogany furniture. The table seated 12. Paintings, including a large landscape over the fireplace, covered the walls. The room led off to a sunroom with French doors overlooking the back grounds and a patio with a statue and fountain in the center.

Sarah's mother sat ramrod-straight at a glass-topped table. She was a thin, hawk-faced woman who looked as if she missed nothing.

"Mom, this is Jack. He's doing investigative work for me and also acting as a bodyguard."

"Do you need a bodyguard?" She displayed a wry smile.

She and Sarah talked about people they knew in the neighborhood and her mother's progress with her painting. Soon, a woman, who I assumed was Rebecca, brought in pastries, fruit, salmon, cheeses and coffee.

"I'm worried about your father," her mother said after

we'd finished the breakfast. "I think he's worried. I don't know what's bothering him. He doesn't share much with me, as you know. I wish he would. I could help him."

"I know, Mom. But you know how Dad is. He's not going to change."

As we neared Murray County on the way home, Sarah asked me to detour to the sheriff's department.

"I want to talk to Shank."

The woman officer at the front desk directed us to his office.

He rose to greet her. "Hello, Sarah." He gave me a side-wise glance that didn't make me feel loved.

"Have you checked out Hal Weaver as a possible suspect in Max's death?" she asked.

"I don't know why you would suspect him," he responded, "but we did. He denied any involvement."

"He could be lying."

"He had an alibi. His wife said he was home that night with her, playing gin rummy."

"That's not the strongest alibi."

"It is when I've got no reason to doubt her."

She frowned. "Well, I won't take up any more of your time."

When we were outside again, I asked her why she hadn't mentioned that Tina thought Weaver was the man who visited her husband that night.

She looked as if she didn't want to answer but then confided: "That's a card I may want to play at the trial, if there is one. That could create doubt in jurors' minds about the prosecution's theories."

35

During the next few days there were no developments. Nothing was coming out of the county courthouse. Charles remained in jail without bond. The neighborhood patrols were continuing but quiet reigned.

On Friday, Sarah flew to Miami for a few days of rest on the beach at the family condo on Fisher Island, heeding her father's advice.

While she was gone, I made a return trip to the Recorder's Office. The numbers in the file allowed me to track down the location of Jennings Development's land holdings. They were scattered in the county, but some were located along the Missouri not far from the marsh.

They were the tracts whose owner I couldn't identify earlier because they were held by a trust.

On Wednesday, Sarah returned to town. She looked tanned and refreshed.

"I did nothing but lie on the beach and read," she said. "And eat some great food in the island's restaurants. You can only get to Fisher Island by private ferry, so you're left alone. I didn't even go to South Beach."

"It must have been relaxing."

"It was."

The next day she learned about the bankruptcy filing. Jennings Development had become a victim of the recession.

Sarah was grim. "I thought this was coming."

For the following several days she spent most of her time on corporation business, conferring by phone with her dad and other board members. She also devoted hours to bolstering her mom, who feared not only that the family would be left with no money and maybe lose their home, but that their reputation and social standing would never recover.

"I don't know what's going to happen to us," Sarah said one evening as we were having cocktails at the house.

She looked more stressed than I'd ever seen her.

The next day she arranged to fly to Kansas City and spend several days with her mother.

She was away when I heard the report on the news. Cliff Jennings, her dad, had been charged with fraud. According to the indictment, he had been kiting checks to cover up the corporation's insolvency.

I tried to phone Sarah but she wasn't taking calls.

A week later, Sarah returned to Little Bend. She told me briefly about her dad's efforts to save the company but said nothing about the indictment.

"He was planning a casino project that he hoped would put Jennings back in the black, but it fell through. I don't know all the details, but it included two hotels and a shopping center. He ran out of time."

Sarah's eyes were dull, her face expressionless. "This is killing my mom."

Sarah didn't ask me to continue to stay with her, but she didn't ask me to go away either. So I went on living at her house.

Much of the time she seemed only half aware of my presence. She didn't go to her office. And almost every time I saw her she had a glass of wine in her hand.

She began to mostly ignore Emily and George. I spent more time with them. Emily became quite affectionate and liked to sit on my lap. George and I played games and explored the far corners of the farm. I also arranged for Cheryl to care for them while I was at the bar. Cheryl also did the cooking but Sarah didn't eat much.

I went to the jail and told Charles what was going on. He felt so bad for Sarah that he didn't mention his troubles.

"Tell her I'm dying inside for her."

When she showed no improvement in the next week, I urged her to see her doctor.

"I'm all right. I need to rest."

I risked arguing with her.

"You're not yourself. You haven't been to the office in over a week. What can it hurt to see a doctor?"

She didn't say anything.

"What you're going through is too much for anyone. You can get help with this. There's no reason for you to keep struggling like this."

When she didn't respond, I stopped pushing her.

That evening—we were relaxing in the family room with Pandora playing cool jazz—she turned to me.

"I think you're right. I'll call Dr. Wright tomorrow."

I took her to her doctor. He referred her to a psychiatrist, who prescribed an antidepressant.

I noticed some improvement after she began taking the medication, though she still was not herself. She began to spend time with the kids again.

"Mom got very sad," she told them, "because Grandpa's in trouble. But everything's better now."

Emily and George listened with rapt attention. They never behaved better.

She thanked me for my support, with a sincerity I'd not seen from her before.

"I owe you. You've been so understanding. I don't know what I would have done without your help."

During this time we talked about the murder case only briefly.

The Actor's party was then only three days away. I could see the effort she was making as she began to prepare for it. But getting out of the house and talking to the other organizers appeared to improve her mental state.

When the evening arrived, I took her to the theater early, then went to the bar to pick up the wine and liquor. The theater made its home in a 150-year-old wooden church building, and the highly polished but uneven plank flooring creaked as I and a waiter from Arnaud's carried in the bottles.

I was relieved to see Sarah chatting with other women setting up the party.

"The season's going well," I heard Kelly say as I set up the bar. "We've already sold out *Guys and Dolls.* "

Sarah walked over to me. "Thank you for doing this for Andre."

"I'm happy to do it."

When Kelly welcomed the guests to the dinner, she thanked them for attending.

"Tonight is an opportunity for all of us to remember our friend Andre," the theater director said. "We at the theater loved him, and we know many of the rest of you did too. His death was tragic and heart-breaking, and all the more so for coming while he was so happy, and full of hope, about his upcoming marriage. But tonight we aren't going to think about that. We are going to remember the happiness and friendship this talented man brought into our lives.

"Recently, a fire destroyed the store that Andre and his partner operated. We think that unique business is part of Andre's legacy. Unfortunately, the insurance isn't covering the loss. We hope Artful Antiques will survive, and the money raised tonight will go to try to make that happen."

Kelly announced that a print donated by Sarah and auctioned off on the Web had brought the highest bid: $4,000. The buyer was Sarah's broker.

"Isn't it incredible?" Kelly asked the crowd, showing off the print to applause.

The pre-dinner entertainment kicked off with the troupe doing a medley of songs from "Cabaret." I had been informed about the program, and in keeping with the musical theme I served "Cabaret" cocktails made with gin and Herbsaint.

Overly coordinated, I knew.

The mood of the guests, with the exception of Sarah, was buoyant when the party began to wrap up. As the last guests walked out, I packed up the unopened bottles. Then I waited to accompany Sarah home.

I didn't know then that the lull in the murder investigation was about to end.

36

On Monday morning, a friend in the state's attorney's office let Sarah know that developer Russ Collins was being called in for questioning in the county corruption investigation.

"Hmm," I said.

"Yes," she responded.

I'd been returning to my house daily again to care for Buddy, but when I turned into my driveway Monday afternoon he didn't come out as usual to shepherd my truck into the yard.

Then I saw Betty waving wildly at me, so I walked down the lane to meet her.

"Someone took Buddy! Put him in his truck yesterday evening and drove away. I didn't know how to find you. He looked like the guy I told you about. The hippie with the pony-tail." Betty's sharp blue eyes fixed me. "I thought you'd want to know."

I jogged back to my house, then phoned Sarah and told her I was going to look for Buddy.

I considered calling the constable but I didn't want to wait for Cudinhead to get a search warrant. That might be too late. Instead I phoned Mike and told him what was up. "I'm going out to Billy's farm. You want to come along?"

"You bet. Come by my place."

I realized that confronting a drug dealer could be risky, but I had Billy sized up as more feckless than dangerous. Just a weak-minded petty crook and user who needed a way to pay for his habit.

In less than three minutes a stern-faced Mike had climbed into my truck cab.

After we veered onto the gravel road leading to Billy's place, clouds of dust billowed behind us. The front and one side of his small one-story house were covered with tar paper, and the porch and grassless front yard were littered with junk including a mangled file cabinet and a stove. Two ramshackle outbuildings stood in the rear. Pigs rooted around in a pen at the side of the closer one.

Out of an abundance of caution I parked on the road out of sight of the house. From there Mike and I threaded our way through brush and a wooded area back toward the farthest outbuilding, where there were dog runs.

All was still. Off to the side of the shed lay a pile of junk that had been burned. Part of the blackened wheel of a retro-style bike stuck out of it.

Mike and I looked at each other.

"You thinking what I'm thinking?" I asked.

Mike nodded.

When I lifted the latch on the shed's side door and pulled it open, thunderous barking erupted.

I looked back at the house but saw no movement.

I turned back to the dusky room, which held dog food, spiked collars, muzzles, lumber chains and other supplies. We entered and found a side door that led to a larger room with what resembled a small circus ring. Dirty and stained carpet covered the ring's floor, and surrounding it was a wooden fence with a gate.

I opened a rear door out of that room and entered a kennel area. Dogs, snarling and barking, began jumping against the wire enclosures of their runs.

Buddy was lying in the last one. He lifted his head and tried to get up but couldn't manage it.

"Buddy, old boy," I said. He thumped his tail a couple of times. One of his ears was half severed, and there were bite marks and blood on his nose and head and a deep, bleeding gash on his shoulder.

"You'll be OK. We'll get you out of here."

I pulled a gunny sack down from a rafter, and, using it as a blanket, carried Buddy outside. After looking again at the house and seeing no activity, we made our way back to the truck.

"I'll drive," Mike said.

I got into the passenger seat carrying Buddy.

"Go to Doc Burk's."

When the animal clinic's receptionist saw Buddy's condition, she got the veterinarian at once.

"What happened to him?" Jim Burk asked as he led the way to an examining room. The veterinarian took out a syringe and began filling it with pain killer.

"He was put into the ring with a pitbull, or pitbulls."

"Let me guess. Billy's place?"

"Right."

"Why the police don't do something about that operation I'll never know."

Then he said: "This will take a while. I'll have to do surgery. If you wish you can wait outside, in the waiting room."

I phoned Sarah but the call went through to her voice mail. I left her a message.

An hour and a half later, Burk came out.

"Well, I stitched him up. He'll have some scars, and his ear may not hang down quite the same way. One of his front legs and one of his back legs were fractured. Those fighting pitbulls have powerful jaws. I put splints on the legs. "I'd like to keep him here for a few days," the vet said, "to make sure no infections develop. His recovery will take weeks. But the good news is he will recover."

I turned to Mike. "A beer?"

"Make it whisky," he said.

Dispatcher Darrell Weaver manned the desk when Mike and I stopped at the sheriff's office. I asked for the detective.

"What can I do for you boys?" Shank asked in a neutral voice after he came out of his office. He was in his shirt sleeves and wearing a shoulder holster.

I answered. "There's a bicycle in a junk pile up at Billy Hatcher's farm that looks like Andre's."

"What the heck were you doing up there?"

"Not what you're thinking."

I told him about Buddy and the pitbulls.

"I wanted to talk to Billy about something else too. I think he broke into my house a couple of weeks ago."

"That was a dumb idea. You should leave the police work to us."

The detective continued: "Well, I'll need to get a search warrant. We can't go around trespassing like you do. Can you meet us up there in an hour and show us this bike?"

Mike and I were parked again on the road, listening to the chatter on the scanner, when the two sheriff's cruisers pulled up behind us.

Shank walked up. "We're going in. Stay back out of the way."

As the detective stepped onto the porch, red sky rimmed the western horizon like a scarf blowing in the breeze.

He pounded on the door.

"Police!"

Dogs inside the house barked fiercely, setting off more wild barking in the kennels in the back as well. The detective moved to the side of the doorway with his Glock service weapon drawn. The deputies had their leg guns up and ready.

Shank knocked again, and a dog slammed itself against the door, barking with rage. After waiting a minute, the detective kicked in the door, which splintered and swung open. A black dog leaped out at them. A deputy shot it in midair, and it fell to the porch with blood coming from its mouth.

Mike and I then stepped up onto the porch as well. I looked past the police and stopped. Billy was lying on the floor a few feet inside the room with blood oozing from a head wound. A second dog snarled and slipped out the door. A putrid ammonia odor flooded out, causing one of the officers to cough.

An M-16 rested against the doorway and a luger lay on the floor near Billy.

"Guess it's good we didn't go to his home earlier," I said to Mike.

Shank bent over Billy's body to check for a pulse.

"He's still alive." The detective moved quickly to summon an ambulance.

"Get a towel," he told a deputy.

The deputy went off to the bathroom and returned with a filthy green towel.

"We can't use that," Shank said.

He took off his jacket and pressed it against the wound.

The deputies began checking the other rooms in the

shack.

"Only a couple of mattresses with mangy blankets," one of them told Shank when they returned. "He must have a roommate."

I looked around the room. Once a kitchen, the space crawled with plastic tubing, some suspended from the ceiling and running to glass jugs and beakers in the grimy sink and on the open oven doors of two crud-encrusted stoves. A propane tank, a bottle of muriatic acid, a bag of rock salt and household cleaners also lay on the floor, surrounded by trash, including cold-medication packages.

"This is one meth lab that won't be doing any more business," the detective remarked.

He looked down at Billy, whose arm had twitched.

Shank asked where the bicycle was and I pointed in the general direction of the shed.

"We'll go look at it once the medics take him away," the detective said, referring to Billy. "Let's step outside. It stinks in here."

We heard the helicopter before we saw it. The clacking of its blades swelled until the sound was deafening. Dust rolled in like fog, enveloping the porch as the air ambulance landed in the field at the side of the house.

"I don't think he's going to make it," I remarked to Jack.

Three paramedics entered the house with a stretcher.

"Let's stabilize him," one said. He checked the patient's pulse. A second paramedic began applying a tight bandage on the wound.

"We got a white male, maybe 25 years old, GSW in the head," the first paramedic radioed. "We have a pulse, weak and thready, but there."

The second paramedic was now inserting a breathing tube while the third one was preparing the C-collar.

"This guy's bad. I hate these gunshot wounds."

They boarded Billy, then put him on the stretcher. As they began to carry him out, the supervisor radioed: "ETA 30 minutes. Have OR ready."

I followed the paramedics out, stopping on the porch. A large pickup truck was slowing in front of the house, as if it was about to turn in, but instead it drove on, accelerating fast.

I saw movement in the woods.

"Someone's out there!" I called out to Shank, pointing to a grove of trees.

The detective summoned the deputies with a shout, "Hey, let's go." But they were back before long.

"He had too much of a jump on us," Shank said. "Did you get a good look at him?"

I shook my head. "He was in the shadows."

Shank scowled. "Probably a drug user. It would be fine with me if all these druggies shot each other."

The constable arrived, and he trailed along as I led the way to the burn pile. A deputy pulled out the bent-up bike.

"That's Hadley's bicycle. I'd swear to it," Cudinhead said.

"No one else has a weird bike like that."

When we entered the kennel area, the dogs began to growl and bark again. One of the runs held a bitch and five puppies. Most of the adult dogs bore scars.

One snarled menacingly as the officers looked them over.

"I'm glad they're locked up," the constable muttered.

"We'll call the Humane Society," Shank said. "They'll take the dogs and check them out. They can adopt out the puppies, but I doubt if they'll be able to save any of the mature ones."

A deputy taunted one of the dogs, which leaped and crashed into the gate.

"Holy shit," he said.

I phoned Sarah to tell her what had happened. She was back in her office.

"Unbelievable!" she said. "You should have let me know where you were going. How's Buddy?"

I told her about his condition when we found him.

"That's awful. Will he be all right?"

"The vet took him into the surgery. He'll recover."

Then she turned to Billy's shooting.

"Who shot him?"

"We don't know."

"Will he live?"

"We don't know that either. He's in ICU."

"You've had some day. This sounds like a game-changer."

Maybe the silver lining in these developments, I thought as I ended the call, was that they might take Sarah's mind off her family and business troubles. If only for a while.

Half an hour later she phoned back.

"I talked to the prosecutor. He'd just heard of the shooting. He hasn't had time to absorb this development."

She had also talked to Charles.

"I asked him if he knew any reason Billy might have killed Andre. He said, 'Only bigotry or plain meanness.' As far as he knew Billy and Andre had never had any contact."

"Could Andre have bought drugs from Billy?"

"I asked him that. But he said Andre never used drugs. He had seen what they did to kids in his neighborhood."

37

For three days, until Thursday, we awaited word on Billy's condition. The sheriff placed a guard on his hospital room 24 hours a day. He assumed that someone else was at least as interested in Billy's health as he was.

In the meantime, Sarah was on the phone again for hours each day, conferring with lawyers for her father and Jennings Development.

"How does it look for your dad?" I asked, hoping that she would take the question in the spirit in which I intended it: a show of interest and concern, not prying into her family's affairs.

She hesitated. "Not good. The case is technical and involves complicated finances, however, so his lawyer may be able to persuade a jury that there was no intentional violation of the law. Dad maintains he's not guilty."

I noted that she didn't say he was innocent.

Now that Sarah was back at work, my routine was to

follow her to Columbia to make sure she arrived safely at her office, then spend the day on my own until I went to work. After my shift ended, I returned to her house to remain overnight. Then on Thursday morning, with no change in Billy's condition, rather than dismiss me after the drive into Columbia she asked me to come into her office to talk.

"Hold all my calls," she told Connie as we walked in.

Once in her office, she poured us each a cup of coffee, then sat against the side of her desk.

"We're treading water on our investigation," she said, "and I'm not happy about that. It seems likely that Billy killed Andre, but I'd bet someone put him up to it. Billy may recover, but he may not too, in which case we'll be stuck where we are now—with some interesting leads but that's all. I want you to brainstorm about how we move forward."

She then dismissed me. No surprise, considering how preoccupied she was with her family's problems.

The young woman at the front desk of the veterinary clinic gave me a smile that communicated her empathy for me as the owner of an injured pet.

"How's he doing?"

"He's doing OK. He's still hurting, but we've got him on pain medication. Do you want to see him?"

"Yes."

I followed her to a back room. Buddy was lying down, with splints on two of his legs, and a bandage around his head and on his shoulder. He looked sedated and didn't try to get up. But he recognized me and rapped his tail on the floor a couple of times.

"Hey, champ, you're looking better. They taking good care of you?"

He thumped his tail a couple of more times, and I stroked him for a while.

"Thanks," I told the aide, and the sentiment was heartfelt. "I'll stop in again tomorrow morning."

But, as it turned out, I wasn't able to do that.

38

I was driving back to Little Bend the next morning when the black truck appeared in my rearview mirror. It followed me until the big curve before Max's house, when a gunshot rang out. My pickup began to ride roughly, and I had to brake to regain control. The truck then forced me into the ditch, causing a crash that threw me forward onto the steering wheel and knocked me unconscious.

When I came to and recovered from the shock, I pulled out my phone and called a wrecker. I also phoned the sheriff's department to report the incident. I recognized the dispatcher's voice. Darrell Weaver.

"Are you injured?"

"Not seriously. I lost consciousness for a bit."

"Do you need medical care?"

"No."

"Is your vehicle badly damaged?"

"It's in bad shape. Besides the flat tire, a fender is smashed in. It's going to need body work."

"Well, it doesn't sound serious enough to send anyone out." Really, I thought. "Come in when you can and file a report."

I hitched a ride to town with the wrecker then rented a car.

"Do you want a drink?" Sarah asked when I got to her place that night.

"That's just what the doctor ordered."

I told her why.

"Are you sure you're all right? You should have gone to the emergency room. You could have a concussion. I'll take you there now."

"No, all I've got is a headache. I'm okay."

"I wish you would let me do this for you, but I can't force you. Do you want to lie down? I could bring you something to eat?"

I was touched by her solicitousness but said, "No, I'm fine."

"Did you see the driver?"

"It was same heavy-set guy. I didn't get a license number. I was too busy trying to keep my truck on the road."

"You could have been killed.

"I suppose. You were right to be afraid of what this guy might do." Let's both be on guard. It won't help Charles if we end up dead."

"It might actually. They would realize that whoever is behind this violence couldn't be Charles. He's still in jail."

"Well, getting ourselves killed is too high a price."

Now it was my turn to be determined to continue the investigation. This thug had gotten under my skin. "I'm not fond of danger, but I plan to press on." I meant even if she pulled out.

She didn't argue the point.

The next morning my head was throbbing and my rib cage was killing me. I could hardly get out of bed. But I stretched as best I could and managed to get dressed.

When I came downstairs, Sarah was talking to her mother. From listening to Sarah's end of the conversation I understood the Jenningses were discussing whether they should put their Kansas City home and the villa on the market.

"I want to keep the farm," she told her mother firmly.

Sarah made us breakfast. I did my best to disguise how sore I was. I followed Sarah in the rental car until she was safely at her office, then went to the sheriff's office in Marseille and filled out the accident report.

The detective came out to talk to me.

"We want to find this guy," Shank said, "but you aren't giving us much to go on. Call us if you see him or his truck again. We'll be there quickly."

He apparently didn't remember that he'd blown me off when I did that weeks ago, but his change of heart was welcome.

39

On Monday, Sarah had an appointment to talk with the attorney general about his probe of the county commission. I tagged along.

She came out alone in less than a quarter of an hour.

"He confirmed the investigation but not whether they've questioned any commissioners. He won't release any information unless there are charges."

After shadowing Sarah on her way to her office, I drove to Marseille, a tedious route through miles of brown farm fields. Upon arriving at the county building, I went first to the office of the county collector, who wasn't in. I moved on to the county assessor's office.

I told him I was an investigator looking into rumors of corruption in county operations.

"I am unaware of any 'irregularities,' as you put it." His smile suggested he thought I was naïve.

There was no point in pressing him.

The county clerk said she had no time to talk to me.

"Well, if you're too busy today, perhaps you could see me tomorrow."

She looked annoyed but agreed.

"Okay, you can come here at 10 o'clock, but you have to keep it short."

I took a break, went to a coffee shop across the street, and ordered a scone and an espresso.

Feeling refreshed, I walked to the office of the recorder of deeds, an elderly man with scoliosis. He appeared to welcome a visitor. It was easy to imagine that his job was boring.

"Come into my private office."

"Been recorder long?"

"Nineteen years."

"You must be popular with the electorate."

"No one else wanted the job." He smiled with amusement.

I told him why I was there. "I keep hearing rumors about questionable practices around here."

"I don't know much about what's going on. I'm not one of the inner circle."

"Surely you must hear things."

"I don't know how true they are. There's a lot I don't know. Hal Weaver calls the shots, and mostly I stay away from him." He smiled. "Safer that way."

But then he became talkative. I realized that, despite his

demurrals, he wanted me to know he was aware of what was happening.

"The biggest hubbub was when my predecessor disappeared without a trace. The police concluded he left to get away from an unhappy domestic situation. But some people didn't believe that. They thought Hal had caused him to 'disappear' because he knew too much about how some prime development sites were acquired."

Then came the disclaimer. "But I don't know if there was any truth to that."

"I hadn't heard about that. What else do 'people say'?"

"Well, they wonder how he got the money to build that house on the river. And to buy that fancy boat. And those cars."

I knew Hal drove a Range Rover, and I'd also seen him in a Jaguar.

"And how do they think he got the money?"

"I don't know if anybody knows. They just know that one year he was living in a modest home here, with an accounting agency that brought in enough for an ordinary lifestyle, and the next he'd built that Taj Mahal and seemed to have more money than he knew what to do with."

"Just keeping up that house would bankrupt most people," I remarked to keep him talking.

The recorder smiled, his eyes twinkling. "It costs less when county work crews help maintain it."

I was early for my appointment with the county clerk the next day. She opened her office door at 10:10 and nodded for me to enter. She was youthful compared with the other county officials. Forty-five-ish.

After I told her why I was there, she looked at me in silence. "Anything I tell you I will deny having said."

"That's all right with me."

"Look back over the minutes of the commission meetings when road contracts were approved. They might interest you."

She wouldn't elaborate. But she knew I could take it from there.

I spent the next day researching the commission's minutes. A pattern began to emerge. The same contractor, B&R Construction, got the county road contract every year but the work was never put out to bid. Instead it was approved as a change order on the previous year's contract.

The original contract had been adopted 15 years earlier and was decided by competitive bids.

The presiding commissioner that year, and in all the succeeding years, was Hal Weaver.

After striking that lode, it made sense to do more digging. The building permit for Weaver's home revealed that the contractor was B&R Construction. Its website described B&R as a multi-armed construction business doing residential, commercial and government work.

I headed out there. The company was located in an industrial area in the west end of Marseille. The site was expansive; behind its chain-link perimeter were construction trailers as well as rows of earth-moving and other machinery, including a battery of trucks, ranging from dump trucks to flatbeds. Parked in front of the office was a black two-door Dodge Ram pickup.

I was pretty sure it would have a dent in its front fender.

I had been giving Sarah space to catch up at the office and work on cleaning up the mess left by the bankruptcy. But I needed her attention again.

It was time to focus on the murder case.

40

News that developer Russ Collins was being indicted on a charge of bribery in the factory farm case broke late Thursday afternoon. The sheriff picked him up and held him for the state. Sarah attended the arraignment the next forenoon.

"He was released on bond," she told me. "Things are beginning to happen."

Sarah greeted me with more news that evening in the library.

"Hal wants to talk to me. I agreed to see him at his home at four o'clock on Monday."

That could be the development I was hoping for, but it worried me.

"I don't think you should go to his house."

"Why not?"

"You could be in danger."

"From Hal? He's the presiding commissioner."

"Nevertheless…"

I told her the results of my visits to county officials and what I'd discovered about B&R.

"Good work. Now we're getting somewhere. You're becoming a rather good detective!"

I made a rueful face.

"You still think it's smart to meet with Hal on Monday?"

"Yes. I want to hear what he has to say, and what he thinks we know. But I'm glad I put him off until Monday. That'll give us time to think about the case in the light of this new information."

"I'd like to tail Russ for a while. Let's see what he's up to now that he's charged. I think Hal's working with him."

"I don't know."

"I want to find out who drives that black pickup. There were too many workers around B&R for me to drive in today. But I should be able to get its license number. If that's not a company truck, I should be able to find out who owns it. He should be our guy."

"Okay. But be careful."

"Careful is my middle name."

The next morning, I checked out an economy rental car. It wasn'tgoing to win any races, but its virtue was its ordinariness; no one would notice it.

Russ' office was in a down-at-heels commercial strip that hadn't benefited from city planning. An auto supply store crowded one side and a modest Greek restaurant flanked the other.

If Russ was a deal-maker, he apparently wasn't a successful one.

The only business with traffic was the McDonald's across the street. It had a playground in front, where no children played. I drove in and ordered a cup of coffee from the drive-thru, then parked.

No one went in or out of the office for an hour and a half. Then a newer model red Mustang drove in. Russ got out and went in the front door.

Noon came and I was getting hungry, so I went into the restaurant and got a burger and fries. I finished them, returned to the car, and, to stave off boredom, flipped on the radio. I heard the news at the top of the hour twice.

Then Russ came out.

I followed as he drove in the direction of downtown, staying several cars back. When an upcoming traffic light turned yellow, Russ gunned his car through the intersection and I lost him.

Discouraged, I went on to B&R Construction and parked near the company's entrance. I was about to abandon that surveillance—it was time for me to be going to Arnaud's—when the black truck drove in. The driver, a large guy with a shaved head parked in front of the office and went in. I drove in and snapped a photo of the truck's Missouri license. I noted its dented fender and Confederate decal.

When I got to the bar, I called the sheriff's department and gave Shank the license number.

"We'll see whose truck it is."

"Can you tell me the name of the owner when you find out?"

"No. This is police business."

"Right."

"How did your surveillance go?" Sarah asked when I arrived home.

I gave an apologetic smile, then said I'd lost Russ. She smiled as if she'd anticipated that.

Sometimes I really didn't like her that much.

The next morning I was back in the McDonald's lot with a cup of steaming coffee. Russ' Mustang was already parked in front of his building. Within 15 minutes he came out and drove off, this time toward the freeway exit. He got onto Interstate 70 and took the Marseille exit. I followed him into the city and to the county government complex then trailed him on foot as he entered the county administrative building and climbed the stairs to the commissioners' offices.

He went into Hal's office.

Half an hour later, he came out with Hal and another man. Cliff Jennings.

I followed them as they drove to the airport and let Jennings out. Russ took Hal back to the county commission offices then returned to his own office, where he remained the rest of the day.

When I got home, Sarah asked for a report on my day. I told her only that Russ had gone to visit Hal.

The last thing she needed was more reason to worry about her dad.

41

The next morning, Saturday, dawned a gorgeous day, with the azure sky shimmering and cloudless. Evil shouldn't exist on such a day. But I knew better. Evil was always around.

I hung around the farm as Sarah collected eggs from the chickens then gave her gelding some exercise. Mel, her hired hand, was there too, mucking out the barn.

I left her to go into Arnaud's in the forenoon to receive a beer delivery and order supplies. I was working at the end of the bar when Cudinhead walked in and strolled over.

"Anything new?" I asked.

"Yeah, Jake is awake and is being moved to the jail."

"His recovery was rapid."

"Yeah. He probably won't recover completely, but the bullet only went through the side of his brain. It did less damage than everyone thought." The constable smirked. "I'm surprised he had a brain."

"So we'll finally find out what he knows?"

"Yeah, probably. Jake wouldn't talk at the hospital. Shank expects to have better luck at the jail. He's interrogating him now."

"You need a confession."

"Shank's a pro. He'll have a guilty plea by tonight. That will wrap up the Hadley murder. It'll end up being an ordinary homicide. A drug dealer punishing a buyer who wouldn't pay up."

"So you don't buy the blackmail theory?

"No. The prosecutor's got an overactive imagination. Shank says that too."

"What about Max's death?"

"Max was drinking. He stumbled and fell off the bluff. Nothing more to it."

"Should be an interesting interrogation."

"You want to watch? I'm going down there now. Shank won't mind."

He didn't have to ask me twice.

That was a break I didn't foresee.

When the deputy let me into the observation room, Cudinhead and another deputy from the investigative unit were watching the interrogation through the one-way mirror. Billy sat slouched, facing us, across a table from the detective. One of his eyes was half-closed and his left arm hung limp.

"How's it going?" I asked.

"Shank's been at it an hour. Nothing so far," Cudinhead said. "He's good at getting crooks to trust him, but this guy's a tough nut."

"They're stopping."

"The doctor has to check him out."

An older man with short grizzled hair entered the room and began examining Billy.

"Okay. He's all right," he said when he finished. "But don't push him too hard. Remember, he's still a very sick man." The doctor had a firm look on his face. "No more than a half hour this time."

Shank noted for the tape recorder, which lay on the table in front of him, that he was resuming the session with the approval of the medical practitioner. The detective, being a clean-cut straight arrow, made a sharp contrast with Billy, whose long and stringy ponytail fell over the bandage wrapped around his head.

He was wearing the jail's jumpsuit.

"You sure you don't want a cigarette?" Shank shook out a Marlboro and held out the pack to the prisoner.

Billy ignored him.

"You know, I can help you," the detective said. "Your life's not easy. I know that. You built up your drug business, and you didn't want it to fall apart."

Billy didn't appear to be listening.

Shank went step by step over the facts, stretching a few possibilities to certainties but staying close to the truth.

"I'll ask for leniency if you cooperate with us. We know

you killed Andre. The bike links you to that. And there's the photo on Andre's camera. You know he got a photo of you attacking him, don't you?"

The detective was bluffing. The specialized crime lab had reported that the photo wasn't able to be used as evidence.

Billy continued looking at the wall, a blank expression on his face.

The detective sat forward, studying Billy.

"You made a mistake. You should have gotten rid of the bike. You know that, don't you?"

Still nothing. Not even eye contact.

"It's a bit warm in here, isn't it?" Though the detective had been relaxed and laid-back when I came in, he now looked tired and on edge. I surmised that the bike was not enough to get a conviction.

"You want a glass of water? How about a Coke?"

Billy again studied the wall.

The detective tried a new approach.

"You didn't do this alone, did you? Someone wanted Andre killed."

For the first time Billy looked up at the detective. But he didn't say anything. The change, however, wasn't lost on Shank. The detective leaned forward and spoke aggressively.

"Someone paid you to murder Andre, isn't that right?"

Billy said nothing and stared again at the wall.

"Who was it? Max?"

Billy shook his head. "He had nothin' to do with it."

"Okay, it was someone else. Who? Does this person want

you to take the rap? You'll pay and he'll get off. Is that the way it'll work?"

No response.

"You know who this person is. Think about him. He's free right now, sitting in a comfortable chair and making plans for his future. I bet he's feeling pretty smart. He's counting on you being dumb. I bet he's hoping you die of your wounds. Then he'd have no worries.

"In the meantime you have no future and may go to death row.

"You know, if you help us, we'll help you."

No response.

"What have you got to lose? We have the evidence right now to lock you up for good. We could get a death sentence. What you did to Andre was nasty."

No response.

"If you tell us who else was in on this, we would recommend a life sentence. Save you from a lethal injection. Who are you trying to protect? This guy can't mean that much to you."

No response.

"Come on," the detective said forcefully. "What do you have to lose?"

Billy looked up again at Shank. "Fuck you."

The detective leaned back in his chair. He looked at Billy for several minutes but said nothing.

"I get being a tough guy who won't cooperate with the police," Shank finally continued. "But you don't want to be a patsy, do you? I'm going to tell you a story. What if the guy you're covering for knew we were coming to pick you up. He got to you first, but instead of warning you, he shot you so you couldn't talk. What about that, Billy? Was he the guy who shot you? Are you afraid he'll finish the job on you if you talk?"

Billy looked over at him.

"You know, we'll arrest him and you'll be safe."

"You'd just fuck me over."

"I know you think that, but you know my reputation. You must know guys who know me. I'm a man of my word."

Billy appeared to be thinking. He shifted in his seat.

"That's what they say about me, isn't it?"

Billy gave a restrained half nod.

"Well, why don't you help me then? I can help you. You shouldn't take the rap for a person who shot you. Someone you trusted."

"Fuck you."

Shank sat back and exhaled. Then he looked at his watch and spoke into the recorder.

"This is Detective Rod Shank and I'm suspending this session at 3:10 p.m."

He snapped the button to turn off the recorder.

42

Sarah told me to wait after I dropped her off at Hal's home Monday afternoon. I had a foreboding about their meeting, however, so when she was nearing the commissioner's house I walked in over the lawn, where I wouldn't be seen, and watched from behind an oak as Hal let her in.

To the left side of the entrance was a flagstone patio with French doors. I snuck up to them and peered in. The room inside was unoccupied. I tried the door handle, and the door opened. Floor to ceiling bookshelves covered two walls, with a sliding ladder in front of one of them. A large tapestry hung on the third wall. I'd seen it before—I remembered the two sheep and shepherd in the corner.

But I was uncertain where.

Then it came to me. It was the tapestry Jennings bought from Artful Antiques. I snapped a photo of it with my phone.

A door to the hall was ajar and I edged up to it. There was the sound of muffled voices. I slipped into the hall and crept in the direction of the voices. They were coming from the rear of the house, from a room whose door was cracked open.

Sarah was sitting in a chair with her back to me. Across from her, the commissioner sat behind a large desk in front of two tall windows. A stuffed pheasant was rising in flight from a bookcase off to the side, and the head of a white-tailed buck protruded from another wall.

"I've heard you and your investigator think the bribery case against Russ is connected to Andre's death," Hal was saying. "Why would you think that?"

"I'm not going to disclose what we know."

"You're wasting your time going down that alley. Russ wouldn't be involved in anything like that. He's a good guy. Those bribery charges were trumped up by the liberals in the state's attorney's office who oppose his projects. You know if these corruption allegations were true, I'd have put a stop to it. We want Murray County to be on the up and up.

"I just don't want you to waste your time."

Just then Hal's phone rang.

"Uh-huh, uh-huh." He listened for a while then I heard him say: "Meet me by the bridge. Yes. You're not listening. That's right."

He put down the phone and opened a desk drawer, then stood up with a pistol in his hand.

Sarah started.

"We have a change of plans. We're going for a boat ride."

I ducked around a corner and watched the two of them exit through a back door and walk in the direction of the river, Hal following with the gun at her back.

I raced out the front door and to my truck, pulling out my cell phone as I ran. I punched in 911.

"Murray County Sheriff's Department."

I recognized Darrell's voice.

"Detective Shank, please."

"He's out."

I wasn't about to tell Hal's son anything. So rather than leave a message I asked for Shank's cell phone number. It was busy. I left a voice mail.

I gunned the truck back to my place and drove up the lane and over my field down to the dock. Minutes later, I was floating at the entrance to the Missouri. I looked upstream but couldn't see a boat. I crossed to the far side, where the shade made my boat less visible and cruised upstream.

Hal's boat pulled out before I reached his property. I cut back on my throttle to stay behind it and reduce my engine noise, though it was being drowned out by the roar of his much larger motors.

I again phoned Shank. This time he answered.

"Shank speaking."

"Hal Weaver has kidnapped Sarah."

"Hal must know that we've got a warrant out for him," the detective said. "Where are they?"

"They're in Hal's boat."

"Where are you?"

"I'm following in mine."

"Good. Stay with them. You have any idea where they're

going?"

"They're heading straight upriver now. I overheard Hal on the phone telling someone to meet him at the bridge. I guess that would be the one outside Paradise."

"We'll head in that direction. Stay behind them, out of sight if you can. He may do something rash if he knows he's being followed."

"Right."

"Keep your phone out. Let me know if he changes course."

Hal appeared to have his skiff running full out. His wash was giving me a rough ride, but my smaller and lighter boat was able to keep up. I could see Sarah in the co-pilot's chair. I tried her number, but after taking the call she ended it without saying anything. I imagined that Hal had ordered her to hang up. I then texted her thinking she might be able to read a message without Hal noticing.

"I'm following behind you," I wrote. "The police are on their way."

Then I sent it. I couldn't tell if she got it.

While I was pursuing, Shank phoned back and explained that Billy had cracked under more questioning and said that Hal shot him.

The time seemed interminable, but it was only about 20 minutes before the Paradise bridge came into view. I now remembered that it was closed and being dismantled. The concrete pylons of a new bridge under construction were pointing up out of the water.

A car ferry was taking traffic across the river.

Hal slowed his boat as he neared the bridge, staying on the Paradise side.

I hung back in the shadows.

"We're up on the highway," Shank said after I'd updated him, "but we're not going down to the river until he pulls into the bank. We want him to take Sarah out of the boat."

"He looks like he's stopping. He's pulling up to the ferry dock."

I could see Hal waving his gun. Then Sarah stepped off the boat. Hal got out too, letting the boat float off.

"They're on the dock," I told Shank.

"We're coming in."

Four squad cars raced down toward the river, raising dust, and then the deputies spilled out of their cars.

Showing signs of panic, Hal forced Sarah up an embankment to the entrance of the old bridge, then motioned for her to go on it. The bridge floor had been removed, so they had to walk on girders.

Shank began directing the deputies. One took a rifle with a scope to a cottonwood by the bank, and two others went to the dock. Then the detective picked up a megaphone.

"Weaver, this is Detective Shank." Shank's voice, magnified by the bullhorn, echoed over the water. "Throw down your gun."

Hal looked down, then the two continued inching along the girders.

"You can't get away. Put down your gun and you won't get hurt."

The order had no effect. The ferry had now returned to the Paradise side and the two deputies got on it.

The detective again raised the megaphone.

"Let Sarah go. If anything happens to her, it'll only be worse for you."

Hal paid no attention.

When the ferry had returned to the west bank, the deputies got off. They pushed their way through the brush to the other end of the bridge.

"You're trapped," the detective shouted. "Give yourself up. There are deputies on both ends of the bridge."

Hal stopped, then shouted down. "Pull the deputies back or I'll shoot her."

Shank spoke into a phone, then picked up the megaphone again.

"I've pulled them back."

Sarah was clinging to a beam. Hal was gesturing at her with his gun. She began to walk again along the girder. They were now at the top of the bridge, about 150 feet above the swirling dark water.

I turned up the throttle just enough to nudge my boat closer to the bridge. The ferry was in front of me, on its way back to the Paradise side. Above me to the left I could see car lights flashing on and off. The vehicle appeared to be stationary.

I was caught off-guard when Sarah plunged off the girder. I heard a gunshot as she was falling. I was moving toward the spot where Sarah had entered the water when I heard another shot and saw Hal also fall.

I scanned the river but couldn't see anything. Then I saw a hand break through the surface and a light-colored form twirling just below it. I was still downriver. So I twisted the throttle, then cut the engine and went to the bow. I caught Sarah's body as it reached the boat.

I struggled to pull her into the boat. With her waterlogged clothing she was surprisingly heavy. Then I turned her over and began administering artificial respiration. Within about ten seconds she began to sputter and spit out water.

"You'll be OK," I told her.

Her eyes focused on me, and she smiled weakly.

I opened a storage box, took out a blanket and wrapped it around her. She was shivering badly, whether from the icy cold water or shock, I couldn't tell. I propped her up against the side of the boat.

"I need to drive us to shore."

She nodded shakily.

The deputies were waiting on the dock, and an ambulance was now on the scene. Two deputies helped Sarah into it.

Shank came over when she was strapped down inside.

"You're going to the hospital," he told Sarah. "They need to check you out. You've been through a lot. You were brave to jump off that bridge."

Shank turned to me after he stepped down from the

ambulance.

"Thank God you were able to fish her out of the river. I thought she was done for."

"What happened to Hal?"

"Our sharpshooter shot him after Sarah jumped. He hasn't surfaced as far as we know. We're searching for him."

I noticed that a police launch with a spotlight was on the river and officers were tramping along the banks with flashlights. It had begun to grow dark.

"We'll find him," Shank said. "Or his body."

43

I climbed into the ambulance with Sarah. On the way to the emergency room I phoned Cheryl, who was caring for the kids, and explained the situation.

"Oh, that's awful!" Cheryl said. "Will she be all right?

"I think so."

"Don't worry about the children. Tell Sarah they're fine. I can keep them here as long as she wants me to."

I had been in the emergency waiting room about an hour when a doctor came out with Sarah.

"Someone should keep an eye on her tonight," he said, "but I think she'll be all right. She's had a shock to her system, but she's in good health.

"Can you drive her home?"

I nodded.

I called Mike and got a ride to my place then went back to the hospital for Sarah. Even during the short time I was away her color had improved. She was strong enough to walk out unaided.

She didn't want any sympathy.

"You were right. I shouldn't have gone to Hal's house."

"Shush."

I helped her into my truck.

"How did you know he abducted me?" she asked as I turned on the ignition.

"I snuck into the house and was watching when he pulled out the gun."

"So you ignored my instructions." She looked stern but then softened. "Considering what happened, I'm glad you did."

We rode in silence for a moment in the dark of the evening.

"I don't think Hal was intending to kidnap me. I wonder why he did?"

"Billy had just told Shank that Hal shot him. The phone call to Hal must have tipped him off. You were his hostage."

"Oh. That call did make him go for his gun. I wondered who called him."

"His son would be my guess. Only someone at the sheriff's office would have known Billy talked."

"Of course. What else did Billy say?"

"I don't know."

"When we were in the boat, Hal phoned someone. That must have been Darrell. I heard him say, 'Flash your lights.' "

I remembered the flashing vehicle lights at the bridge. We were then stopping to pick up George and Emily.

"My guess is that Darrell was supposed to pick up his dad," I said.

When Sarah opened her front door and flipped on the switch, warm and welcoming light flooded the entranceway. The kids and I followed her to the kitchen. She plopped onto a stool at the island.

"Make us both a drink," she said, pointing to the liquor cabinet.

Emily and George, unaware of the seriousness of what had just transpired, began to play on the floor. We were all hungry, and I would have offered to make them chili but I was still smarting from Sarah's putdown.

So instead I offered to get carry-out from Adrian's.

"That would be nice," she said.

"Any requests?"

"Anything. George and Emily like chicken."

When I left the house, I heard Sarah lock the door behind me. When I returned, dinners in hand, Sarah was cautious about re-opening it. She had recovered some of her energy.

"This smells wonderful," she said as she opened the containers.

"What made you jump off the bridge?" I asked.

"I thought Hal would shoot me sooner or later. My chances were better if I jumped. I don't want to ever go through something like that again. Ever. By the way, thanks for texting me. It meant so much to know you were following us."

Later, I accompanied Sarah as she put her children to bed.

"You'd make a good daddy," she said, smiling, as we left

George's room. "I hope you don't mind, but I'm going to go to bed. I'm just beat."

"Well, yeah," I said, rising above my hope that we would sleep together. "That was traumatic."

And, I could have added, you already were coping with all the trauma you could handle.

"Would you mind staying with me in my room tonight?" she asked. "I'm not up for sex, but I would like your company."

"I'll get my pajamas. But first I'll run a tub for you."

She smiled.

"Do I have to go to school?" George asked. It was eight o'clock the next morning, and he had come down for his breakfast.

"You can stay home today," Sarah said.

"All right!" George plunged a spoonful of cereal into his mouth.

I laughed.

"I need to get my boat," I told Sarah. "Can you drive me to the ferry dock."

"Yes."

She poured more coffee into her cup.

"I'm ready," she said. "George, Emily, let's go."

As we rode toward Paradise, an occasional hardscrabble farm or a pasture with scraggly cattle broke up the wild rolling hills and woodlands. Sunlight filtered through the trees, striping the roadway.

"It looks so peaceful," Sarah remarked.

Soon a sign announced "Reduced speed ahead." An abandoned motel appeared along the roadside and then scattered houses at the outskirts of Paradise. We wound through a residential area until the bridge over the river and grain elevators came into view. The quaint downtown spread out behind the towering structures. The detective's car and another squad car were parked in the gravel lot in front of the dock, where a sign read: "$10 per vehicle."

"Shank must still be directing a manhunt," I said. "Or a search for Hal's body."

"I hope Hal isn't alive and around here somewhere."

"I'll see what I can find out."

I walked over to the detective's car.

"Know anything?"

"Not yet." He was now speaking to me with genuine respect. Imagine that. "We've got the roads out of here covered, and deputies are searching the shoreline. We've also got boats going along the shore and a dragging operation under way. The copter is circling the woods too, but we haven't seen anything. We've been here all night."

I walked back to Sarah and relayed what I'd learned.

"Be careful driving back," I said. She looked vulnerable, and I impulsively gave her a kiss, surprising her.

George and Emily looked on, wide-eyed.

The police launch must have retrieved Hal's boat because

it was moored next to mine. I looked it over, admiring it. It was a Carolina Skiff, a 28-footer, I estimated, and powered by two 150-horsepower outboards. With its draft of about a foot it made an ideal boat for the shallow river.

I cast the line off my runabout and pushed out into the current. I took my time as I cruised, letting the sun warm me and watching the deputies at work. I'd gone about two miles when I saw a sheriff's boat and squad cars on the tip of Straggler's Point. I pulled into the bank.

When I got near the circle of officers, I saw a man's body in the water, face down. His shirt was in tatters and his back mangled. It looked like it had been hacked multiple times by a meat cleaver.

Shank had just arrived. "Jeez," he said. "Well, let's get it out of the water."

They dragged the body up on the bank, then turned it over.

It was Hal. He had a bullet hole in his shoulder.

I phoned Sarah.

"Hal's not going to be the boss of anything anymore," I said. I told her about the recovery of the body. "Shank says he must have tangled with the ferry's prop. He apparently was alive when he hit the water."

"Good grief. That is a terrible way to die."

"Yes."

44

Shank phoned the next morning to say he'd arrested the man suspected of intimidating us. He asked Sarah and me to come to the jail to pick him out from a lineup.

We were taken into the room separately. All of those in the lineup were big men, and all but three had shaved heads. Two were bald. But I recognized the guy at once.

Afterwards, Sarah told me she did too.

The detective wouldn't tell us if we had pointed to the suspect. He also wouldn't say whether Sarah and I picked the same man.

Once she'd recovered, Sarah continued working from morning until night. When she wasn't at her law office, she was on the phone to Kansas City consulting with board members, lawyers or her family. She was continuing to take the anti-depressants, but most of the time she again looked either depressed or manic.

Charles' defense was on a back burner. We were mostly waiting to hear what the police were learning from the truck driver, a man named Joe Rizzo.

Unlike Sarah, I had plenty of time to think about the murder. I now had a sinking feeling about where the investigation would lead us.

I hadn't told Sarah about my discovery of the tapestry in Hal's home. Nor had I told her that her father was with the commissioner when Russ visited them at Hal's office. I was now also convinced that the man who had been at the marsh with the developer was the same person.

That's the thing about a good memory. You remember clearly, even when you'd rather not.

I had begun stopping by the Little Bend police station regularly to pass the time with Cudinhead, and that was paying off. I wanted him to keep me updated on the sheriff's probe. He actually showed some signs of liking me.

I didn't like him any better.

One morning he let me know that Rizzo was a known associate of the Kansas City mob.

Nice, I thought. As if local thugs weren't brutal enough.

On Friday, four days after the kidnapping, the constable waved me into his office. "You'll want to see this."

I moved toward the old rattan chair, noticing again the dog hairs, cracker crumbs, bits of grass and oil stains on its cushion. It would have been a find for a rat. I decided to stand.

"The prosecutor offered Rizzo a plea agreement in exchange for his testimony. I think you'll find his statement interesting."

He passed the sheet to me.

I, Joe Rizzo, agree to testify to the following:

1. Acting as the agent of Hal Weaver, I paid Billy Hatcher $500 to kill Andre Hadley.

2. On several occasions I threatened lawyer Sarah Smithson and her investigator, Jack Archer, in attempts to get them to drop their defense of Charles Parker. These threats included intimidating phone calls, following Smithson, and shooting out a tire in Archer's truck and forcing him off the road. The intimidation was arranged by a Kansas City individual, whose identity I am unaware of.

3. On Weaver's orders, I shot up Andre Hadley's apartment to break up his campaign kickoff.

4. Weaver told me he "had taken care of" Max Arnaud after I informed him that Arnaud had been asking me about Weaver and his relationship with my employer, B&R Construction.

After I read the statement, I looked at Cudinhead.

"Does this mean Charles will go free?"

"They're releasing him today."

I asked the constable if he knew any more about the Kansas City "individual."

"Joe only spoke to the man by phone. But he said Weaver was also talking to someone in Kansas City, and that that man was 'the boss.' "

"Is Shank trying to find this man? I assume it's a man."

"Yes. He's a man. We really don't have anything to go on regarding him. Weaver may have been the only one who knew who he was, and Weaver's dead."

That's a break, I thought.

I phoned Sarah. She was aware of Charles' release and was about to go to the jail to pick him up.

She was more upbeat than at any time since the bankruptcy announcement. "We've won! Finally, Charles has this monkey off his back."

She knew about Hal's role in Andre's murder and Max's death, and she knew that Rizzo had given a statement. But she hadn't seen it. I hoped she wouldn't.

We both knew she no longer needed me as her bodyguard. She hadn't asked me to accompany her to the jail.

"I guess it's safe for you to drive home alone now."

"There's no need for you to come for me."

Then, she added, "I'll hold dinner until you get home tonight."

That made me smile. But my smile faded as I realized that this might be our last regular dinner together.

45

When I arrived at her house after work, she greeted me with a kiss.

"Where are the kids?" I asked.

"I packed them off to Cheryl's for the night."

"And Charles?"

"He's staying with a friend in Columbia. I think he wants to celebrate. And he wants something more than a family celebration."

Sarah had cooked a gourmet dinner as a celebration for us. We enjoyed it with candlelight and wine in the dining room.

The topic of my future with her didn't come up. But she did invite me to her bedroom.

"Another irregular occurrence?"

She smiled alluringly.

The next day she phoned me about noon.

"Bill showed me Rizzo's statement. It mentions a Kansas

City 'individual.' "

"I know. I've read it."

There was a silence. "I don't want to talk about that now. Let's talk about it tonight."

She sighed. "I didn't know how cheap murder was. $500 isn't much to kill a man."

"I wouldn't be surprised if Hal forked over more," I said, "and Rizzo took a cut for himself."

Then she passed on the rest of her information. And it was another breakthrough.

"Bill Henry said Billy has admitted to the murder. Since Rizzo informed on him, Billy didn't have much reason to continue holding out."

"No, I suppose not."

"Billy was supposed to make the killing look like a hate crime."

"He managed to do that."

"Yes. Apparently he used his own demented imagination."

That evening, we took cocktails into the sunroom. Our invisible companion was the subject we didn't want to talk about. I wasn't about to open that conversation. So instead I asked about her day.

She seized the chance for delay.

"I had to spend two hours persuading an important

client not to sue a neighbor who trapped her cat and took her to animal rescue. The cat's screeching at night was keeping the neighbor awake."

"Sounds like a profitable case."

She half-laughed. "Can you see me arguing for damages?"

"A cat's pain and suffering should be worth, what? $200,000?"

"You should have been a lawyer."

"Not my line. I'm a detective, don't you know?"

She laughed.

Buddy now came into the room and settled awkwardly by my feet because of the splints on his legs. I'd brought him to her house to keep an eye on his progress after his release from the clinic, and a bonus for him was all the tender attention he was getting from Emily. Buddy and Sarah's dogs were tolerating one another in an uneasy peace.

"Buddy's doing well," Sarah said.

She looked out the dark window and then, in a resigned voice, plunged into the subject we'd been avoiding.

"Since you're the detective, who do you think the 'Kansas City individual' is?"

"I don't know."

"I think you do."

"No, I don't."

"Let me phrase it a different way: I think you have an idea who it may be."

Nice lawyerly move, I thought.

"My ideas don't matter. Let it go. We know who killed

Andre and who pushed Max off the cliff. Hal's dead and Billy's going to prison, if not the gas chamber."

She spoke sternly. "I want you to tell me who you think the Kansas City man is."

"It's only a guess."

"I want to know."

"I think it's your dad."

"Yes."

"You should drop this."

"No, tell me why you think Dad's the man."

"I don't want to do this." I looked searchingly at her, but she remained resolute. "Well, there are some things I haven't told you. I believe your dad and Russ and Hal were partners."

"I want to know the specifics."

I told her about seeing her dad with Russ near the marsh.

"And I saw your dad come out with Hal after the meeting with Russ. The two of them took your dad to the airport."

"I see."

"There's one more thing," I added reluctantly. "When I was in Hal's house the night he abducted you, I saw the tapestry your father bought from Artful Antiques on the wall in Hal's library."

"That could have been a payoff from Dad to Hal."

"Yes."

"And the casino project that Dad was planning…"

I finished her sentence for her. "…was undoubtedly along the marsh. It was a great site."

"Yes."

She knew as well as I that Missouri only allowed gambling on riverboats, though they could be stationary along a riverbank. Casinos, especially ones with the close freeway access this one would have had, were cash machines.

"This is circumstantial evidence and conjecture, as you know."

"It's damning, regardless. We don't have to follow court-room rules of procedure here."

She looked thoughtful. "I have another piece to add, as if the evidence isn't overwhelming enough. Bill said Billy admitted breaking into your house to steal and destroy your notebooks. He said Rizzo arranged that burglary too."

"Hmm."

"Rizzo is a known associate of Kansas City mobsters," I said.

"So he is another Kansas City connection."

Sarah looked intense, almost fierce.

"I need to go to Kansas City and have a talk with Dad." She stared out the window again. "Would you come along again?"

"I'm at your disposal."

46

Charles appeared at the front door the next morning, soon after our breakfast. Sarah let him in.

"I'm departing this burg! I've come to get my things."

"Where are you going?" I asked.

"As the song says, I'm going to Kansas City."

"What are you going to do there?" Sarah asked.

"I'll take some time to think about my future, but I may open Artful Antiques in Crestwood." That was a tony shopping area south of the Plaza. "The money you guys raised may be enough to enable me to begin restocking."

"That would be a good location for you. But I hate to see you abandon the store here and leave us. We'll miss you."

"I know, you're sweet." But then perking up, he added, "But don't get all sappy on me. Help me pack up."

When his suitcases were in the car, he turned to us.

"Well, this is goodbye. I love you guys and owe you so much. I'll never forget the way you stood by me. We absolutely will stay in touch."

"Definitely," Sarah and I said simultaneously. That made us smile at each other.

Charles hugged Sarah then me. He got in his car and waved. Sarah and I watched him drive away.

"I feel like a chapter has ended," I said.

"Yes," she said.

Later that morning, Sarah and I took the kids to Cheryl's and left for Kansas City. She again asked me to drive. Then she put her seat back and put on a sleep mask.

I left her to her thoughts.

When we got into the city, we registered at a Plaza hotel. "I may need to get away from my family," she said.

That afternoon I sacked out while she went to the house to be with her mother. She returned about 5:30.

"Let's have a drink," she said.

We went down to the hotel lounge.

"I'm going to meet Dad for dinner at 7 at the Savoy Grill. I hope you'll come too."

I knew the Savoy. It was an old hotel downtown on the side of a hill rising up from the Missouri and known mostly for its steak and lobster restaurant. The restaurant's ambiance was uniquely Kansas City, with lots of dark wood and murals of a cattle drive and other Western scenes on its walls.

Her dad was seated in a booth when we entered. He was

bent over and staring at the tabletop. When he looked up and saw us, I noted the dark bags under his eyes. He looked besieged and had lost some of his arrogance, but he still conveyed the impression that he was a powerful and influential man.

He gave Sarah a kiss. "We're so relieved you're all right after the kidnapping. You look like you're fine."

"I am now."

"You wouldn't listen to me, but I warned you that you might be in danger there. I'm so glad you're safe now."

Then he held out a hand to me.

"Nice to see you again, Jack. We're very grateful you were there to rescue Sarah."

We sat down and the conversation moved to small talk until the waiter arrived for our drink order. Then Sarah and her dad talked about his legal defense.

"I don't think Mom will ever get over this," she said.

"I know." He looked down. "My judgment was bad. I made mistakes."

There was an uncomfortable silence until the waiter returned. We all ordered the lobster. No one said much as we dutifully picked at the lobster and sweet corn. The dinners were delicious, but none of us was interested in food.

Afterwards, Sarah looked intently at her dad. "You were involved in what was happening in Little Bend, weren't you?"

He toyed with his fork. "What makes you ask that?"

"Just tell me. Were you working with Russ Collins and Hal Weaver?"

"We had talked about doing some projects together."

"And you were planning a casino on the riverbank."

"That's one of the ideas we had thrown around."

"Did you know that Hal arranged Andre's murder?"

Her father just looked at her.

"Yes."

"Dad, just who were you in business with? Did you know what kind of men these guys were?"

"Sarah, you've been sheltered from the real world, but I have to live in it. I did what I thought had to be done to keep our corporation successful. I couldn't be a Sunday school teacher and continue to assure that you and your mom would have the best of everything."

"Did you have anything to do with these deaths?"

"No, of course not."

"I don't believe you," she spit out.

Her dad just looked at her.

"Did you order the break-in at Jack's home?"

"No."

Sarah appeared to have a sudden and shocking thought. "You didn't hire Joe Rizzo to try to scare us off the case?"

"Sarah, I tried to convince you to leave those cases alone. You didn't know what you were digging into."

She was angry now. "You could have gotten me killed!"

"I told him not to hurt you."

"Dad, he was a mobster!"

She paused. "I don't want to know who else you've been associating with. I'm going now...."

"Sarah, please..."

"I don't know what I'm going to do. But don't call me or visit me. If I ever want to see you again, I'll call you."

She turned to me. "Let's go."

47

"I need another drink," Sarah said as we left the Savoy. "Let's go to Pierpont's."

I maneuvered through the clogged downtown streets, past the glitter of the Power and Light District and the pearl-gray shell of the Kauffman Center for the Performing Arts, from whose wall of windows a hazy light emanated. I normally would have found the view inspiring, but now I hardly noticed it.

I only thought about the agony of the beautiful woman sitting next to me.

Our footsteps echoed on the marble floor of the largely empty hall of Union Station. We walked downstairs to the restaurant, and Sarah moved to the bar and took a stool.

"I imagine you're getting tired of holding my hand," she said.

"Hardly."

I was telling the truth too.

"Dad was the man behind the curtain, directing every-thing. You know that, don't you?"

I nodded.

"Whenever he's involved in something, he's in charge," she said with conviction.

We sat there, sipping our drinks without saying much. Finally we went back to our hotel.

We got up before eight the next morning. I wondered if Sarah had slept at all. We packed and were on the road in half an hour. Breakfast was at a McDonald's on the way home.

"I've got some thinking to do," she said.

She didn't explain for two days. When she came home on Monday—I was off that day—she said, "I've made my decision."

"About what?"

"Dad."

"What is it?"

"I need to tell the police what we know about him."

I looked at her. "Are you sure you want to do that?"

"I am. It's wrong to conceal evidence of a crime, especial-ly one as serious as murder."

"You could be putting your father in prison for life. Can you live with that?"

"I can't live with shielding him. It's not right that he should escape the consequences of his actions."

"You know, your father's already been punished. He may go to prison over the check-kiting. And he's lost everything that's most important to him. His reputation, his corporation and, maybe the biggest loss of all, you. And think of the innocent people who would be hurt. Your mother and the rest of your family. They've already gone through so much humiliation."

"I know that."

"Even with the information we could give the police the state probably wouldn't be able to convict your father. We don't have hard evidence. Hal, and maybe Russ, are the only witnesses, and Russ isn't going to talk and Hal's dead."

"You may be right. I'm going to just tell what I know and let the legal system take over. If Dad is convicted of murder, so be it. HE SHOULDN'T BE SPARED. HE DID TERRIBLE, EVIL THINGS!"

She shouted the last sentence, and I stopped talking.

"The rest of us Jennings shouldn't be spared either. We enjoyed the rewards of his actions. I have to do this, for myself and my family. It's the beginning of our penance."

I didn't know what she was talking about.

"It's the only way we can regain our family's honor."

That I understood. I had never admired her more.

She picked up her phone and tapped out a number.

"Dad, I wanted you to know first. I'm going to the police tomorrow and tell them what I know."

Then she hung up.

She never took that dreadful action, however.

Early the next morning, she received a call from her aunt. When she put the phone down, her face looked drained of blood and her eyes were unseeing.

"What is it?" I asked.

"Dad's dead."

"What happened?"

"He shot himself."

I went to hold her and she collapsed in my arms, sobbing. After a few moments, I helped her to a chair.

"I killed him. I drove my father to his death."

"No, you didn't."

"I did. I should have listened to you. Why am I always so certain I'm right?"

"You did do the right thing. You should be proud of that."

She just looked at me, expressionless.

I didn't know what to say.

When I brought in *The Kansas City Star*, a headline on the front page read: "Developer found dead of a gunshot wound." A deck added: "Revolver lay on bed next to body."

"I have to go home to Mom," she said. "You can stay here." She seemed distracted. "I am just happy she doesn't know everything I know."

Sarah stayed in Kansas City through the funeral on the following Monday. While she was gone I watched the kids. She was somber when she returned to Little Bend but no longer depressed. She became attentive again to Emily and George and took them on walks around the farm.

She also was away for hours alone on her horse.

Then, at breakfast on Thursday, she said:

"I feel strangely free. Freer than I've ever felt before. I no longer have to live up to being a 'Jennings.' No one wants to be a Jennings now. And now that I'm no longer rich, I can be myself. I don't owe anybody anything.

"I can be nobody. It feels so good."

I quoted some lines from the Emily Dickinson poem:

I'm nobody! Who are you?
Are you nobody too?
How dreary to be somebody!

She smiled, showing surprise at the literary reference.

As I watched her, I thought: Our relationship was now different. A distance between us had shrunk, then disappeared.

"You've changed," I said.

"Is that good?"

"Yes. But I liked you the way you were too." I smiled. "Most of the time."

She laughed "You've changed too. Or maybe I just know

you better. You seem more mature, and I like that."

I thought about all we had been through together, all the shocking happenings over a span of just weeks.

"I'm sorry if I have become too serious. I'll try to correct that."

She laughed again.

"Why don't you make us chili for lunch?"

The day was unseasonably warm, with a light breeze, so we decided to eat outside. The spring sunlight cast its radiance over the rippling new grasses in the rolling fallow field adjacent to us. It was scored by darker ravines, which were lush with vegetation, ranging from hackberry, walnut, silver maple and sumac to oak. Behind us were the farm's weathered outbuildings, where the past lingered, mingling with the present, giving the scene a rich complexity.

I said, "I guess you no longer need an investigator. All the mysteries are solved."

"For now. We made a good team."

I liked the way she avoided a note of finality. That emboldened me to go on.

"Do you and I have a future?"

"Are you sure you want to spend more time with me. I am an older woman."

"Just answer one question: Do you think the 'irregular occurrences' might happen more often?"

"I think they might become regular."

Then she added: "Despite what you say, you must have grown weary of seeing me through all this drama."

"I told you 'no' before, and I meant it." I looked at her to reinforce my words. "I love you, you know."

She took a moment to absorb that. "I know I want us to go on living together. I can't think further than that right now."

I heard what she didn't say. But her response was enough. Being with her was enough.

I was smiling like a goof as we ate more chili.

"I guess I'll go get more of my things," I said when our bowls were empty.

She looked up at me and smiled.

I caught myself whistling as I strolled to my truck.

"Here comes the sun, it's all right …"

Acknowledgements

I want to express special thanks to Col. (Ret.) John Archer, Jay Watts and Bonnie Shaw, Marianne Horchler, Ben Gardner, the Rev. Marshall Singletary, Carolyn MacDonald, Mike Firesmith, Homer Pankey, and Walter and Brenda Thomson for their inspiration, support and gentle criticism; to my daughter Dr. Brit Kinney and brother Stephen Anderson for their suggestions that made me appear much more knowledgeable than I am about emergency medical procedure and weaponry; to the Quitman, GA Police Department for information about special operations procedures; and to my friend Sue McFadden, the talented designer of this book.